ANYONE BUT YOU

BRIEN MICHAELS

RIPTIDE
PUBLISHING

Riptide Publishing
PO Box 1537
Burnsville, NC 28714
www.riptidepublishing.com

Anyone But You

Cover art: L.C. Chase, lcchase.com/design-portfolio.html
Editors: Grace Stack, Veronica Vega, Carole-ann Galloway
Layout: L.C. Chase, lcchase.com

ISBN: 978-1-62649-891-4

First edition
December, 2019

Also available in ebook:
ISBN: 978-1-62649-890-7

ANYONE BUT YOU

BRIEN MICHAELS

RIPTIDE PUBLISHING

For Sue, Elizabeth, and Melissa, who encouraged me to keep at it when I thought this book was garbage. For Katie, who is one of the kindest people I know. For my Little Monster, who's still trying to find his way. And for Silk, because I wouldn't want to do this with anyone but you.

TABLE OF CONTENTS

PROLOGUE

R yan hated doing his makeup at the club. De-dragging was one thing, but he liked to focus when he was painting his face, and having half a dozen other people running in and out around him made that a little difficult. But the Owens' case had kept him at the office longer than he'd wanted, so he had to do what he had to do. He slid the wig cap into place, twisted the top off his glue stick, and started gluing down his brows.

Usually, unless he had something special planned, he let his hands do the walking and let the final product be a surprise. Tonight, he wanted a more classic feel. Something understated, more woman than queen. Something that might make Jack take a second look.

Woah.

Where the hell had that come from? He blinked himself back to reality, noticed he'd overdone his nose contour, cursed under his breath, and wiped it away before starting again. Already his mind was wandering, back to Jack, the associate they'd hired at the office a few summers ago. Jack was attractive, sure. And yeah, Ryan might have wanted to drag him into the copy room and show him how all the buttons worked. Once or twice. But the first rule of being a good boss was you didn't fuck your subordinates. No matter how much you wanted to.

And he really wanted to. A few weeks ago he'd gone down to the gym on the second floor of their office building to grab a quick shower before his show and found Jack on the weight bench, muscles bulging and body glistening. It had been nearly a full minute before Ryan had realized he was staring. Mouth dry, Ryan had dipped out of sight as Jack dropped the bar back into the cradle with an audible grunt of relief.

Ever since then, Ryan had seen Jack all over the office, like Jack had been following him. He'd even thought he'd detected a hint of flirting, but it was probably all in his mind. Even if it wasn't . . . he could never go there. Career suicide, party of one.

That didn't stop Ryan from wondering what Jack looked like out of those clothes, though, as he beat his face with setting powder and let it do its thing.

He pulled on his outfit for the night, then spun this way and that in the mirror, making sure the sequins still caught the light the way he wanted.

There was a knock at the door, and he turned, raising an eyebrow. The queens in this club didn't usually knock. They barged in, got what they needed, and left. "Come in?"

Justine poked her head in. Her wig looked like a giant beehive, yellow, streaked with white and little patches of black every few inches going up.

"Just wanted to check in and tell you to kill it tonight."

Ryan smiled at the queen who'd put him in drag for the first time. "Don't I always?" Justine blew a kiss and backed up.

There was a thud from the hallway, followed by Justine's disgusted grunt. "Can you watch where the fuck you're going?" Then the *click clack* of heels, and she was gone.

Valentine appeared in the doorway, glaring back the way she'd come. "God, I can't stand her. Always walking around like she owns the place just because she's been around since before the bug walked."

Ryan smirked. "You two need to fuck already and get it over with." He inspected himself in the mirror. Satisfied, he pulled his wig from the foam head and pinned it into place.

Sheila was making her appearance once more, and it was time to give her adoring fans what they wanted. "See you, bitch," she said to Valentine, giving her an air kiss.

She left the dressing room and headed for the stage.

CHAPTER ONE

Thinking with your dick was never a good idea. Jack had learned that back in high school, but he'd stopped using his upstairs brain to think as soon as Sheila shimmied on stage, sequins glimmering in the club's overhead lights. The drag queen's set had started with a slow, sultry song that'd gotten Jack's pulse racing, and now, she was doing acrobatics on a pole one of the bouncers had wheeled out for her. Fuck, he needed to get laid.

And he hoped Sheila would help him with that. She jumped off the pole and landed in a split, grinding against the ground to the beat of one of Britney Spears's early hits. Jack swallowed. He couldn't tear his gaze away from the queen. Her face was mostly makeup, that was clear, and she was still one of the most beautiful people he'd ever seen. There was something familiar about her, as well, though. He couldn't put his finger on why, but he felt like he'd seen her before. The horndog in him wanted to get closer. Wanted to know more. Wanted to know if she'd do a split like that on his cock.

He took a few steps forward, pulled some ones from his back pocket. Everyone else had thrown their bills on the stage, but he wanted her to know that these were from him. He sidled up to the edge and shook the dollars to signal her. She looked down, faltered for half a second. He wouldn't have even noticed if he hadn't been watching so intently. A heartbeat later, she was back on routine. She sank to her knees and crawled to him, eyes practically screaming *Fuck me!* as she lip-synched.

Her face was nearly in his crotch before she straightened up and gestured for him to stick the money in her cleavage. He did as instructed. Their eyes met and he licked his lips. He wanted to follow her to her dressing room, bend her over the vanity, and not stop until she saw stars. But that would be creepy. He couldn't go back there, uninvited. Maybe if he had a chance to talk after the show, he could charm her and she'd invite him. Yeah. That's what he'd do.

She winked and climbed to her feet, giving her ass a little shake before strutting off to the other side of the stage.

He needed a drink. A cold shower. Anything to take his mind off her. He couldn't tear himself away, though. He stayed rooted to that spot until she took her final bow.

"My name is Sheila Saltue," she said in a false, chipper voice, "and I'm here every weekend. Thank you all for coming!" She busied herself collecting the rest of the dollar bills as the club's own music blared through the speakers and the crowd surrounding the stage started to disperse.

Jack looked around. While Sheila had been on, a red glow had filled the club, adding to the allure of her performance, but now it was just a room again. Dance floor right behind him with couples here and there, grinding against one another to whatever song was playing. The bar was on the other end of the floor, crowded with people getting their liquid courage for the night. The bartender was flustered already. Jack scanned the balcony above them. A few people leaned against the railing, but everyone was absorbed in their own conversations. Which meant that no one was paying attention to him.

This was his chance. Jack approached the stage, throat suddenly dry. His dick strained against the fabric of his boxers, and he'd go insane if he didn't find some relief soon. If he couldn't hit it off with Sheila, he'd beat off in the bathroom and then head home.

She looked up at him, and there it was again, that flash that something wasn't right, but as soon as it had appeared it was gone. So fast he wondered if he'd imagined it.

"Hello," he said, a little more hoarsely than he liked, so he cleared his throat and tried again.

Sheila smiled, a thousand-watt gleam that made her even more gorgeous. "Hey, handsome."

Jack dared to take a step closer so they wouldn't have to shout to hear each other over the music. "I'm Jack," he said, holding out his hand, which she took in a surprisingly strong grip. "I really enjoyed your show."

Her smile became a grin. "I could tell. You almost put my eye out with that thing." She gestured at his crotch, and it took everything in him not to cover it. He shouldn't have worn the sweats. "I'm Sheila. It's nice to meet you."

They stood in silence for a full five seconds before Sheila nodded and went back to collecting her pay. Jack racked his brains for something, anything to say, but he couldn't think straight. His brain wasn't working at all, but he couldn't let her leave without trying.

He took a seat on the edge of the stage, still trying to figure out his next move. This was so stupid! What had he been thinking?

That you wanted to fuck a man before you're thirty, and since you're too much of a chickenshit to just do it, a drag queen is the safer bet. Since, you know, they at least look *like women.*

He hated the part of his brain that answered questions he hadn't actually asked. But it wasn't wrong. Not really.

"Well, I've gotta run, cutie, but I'll see you around. Come check me out again." She turned and headed for the steps.

"I was thinking about trying to get into doing drag," he said, inventing wildly. "Could you maybe give me some pointers?"

She paused, spun around, and met his gaze again. "Have you now?"

No. He absolutely had not. "Yeah. But I don't know how to do makeup or anything about wigs or dresses or stuff like that."

She shot him a skeptical look. "You should maybe get a crash course in all that, first."

"Yeah. I was hoping maybe you could help me."

She appraised him for a moment. She didn't seem to buy what he was selling but, right when he thought she was about to dismiss him, she jerked her head in the direction of a corner shrouded in shadows. "Follow me."

His heart pounded as he tailed her down a hallway. Posters advertising different drag competitions lined the black walls. Red lights shined down on them from little circles in the ceiling. Jack couldn't take his eyes off the queen, though; the way she filled out the skirt she wore, the glimmer of her top. Even her fucking pantyhose sparkled.

They turned a corner, and he could see a door set into the far wall. The closer they got, the harder his pulse beat. Maybe this was a mistake. Underneath all that foundation, Sheila was still a man. Jack had never been able to keep it up when he'd tried to fuck a man before, so why should this time be any different? They always got him hard in the beginning, and God, he always *wanted* to fuck them, but he'd get to "go" time, and everything would go to shit. Every time, without fail, he'd imagine his parents, or his fucking brother, or one of the other homophobic assholes in his family (*Cal*), and he'd go soft in an instant. What would they think of him if they knew what he was doing?

He wanted to turn and run before he embarrassed himself again, but sheer determination kept him following. He would try, because he couldn't go his whole life refusing himself his desires. If it worked, it worked. If it didn't, it didn't.

They made it into the dressing room at last, and Sheila shut the door behind them. This was nothing like he'd imagined. He'd pictured a large, expansive space with a line of lit vanities and mannequin heads topped with wigs and rows and rows of dresses and heels. But this was almost exactly the opposite. It was hardly bigger than his bathroom at home. There was only one mirror perched atop a rickety-looking table and a large rolling rack to the right of it. On the tabletop were a few palettes of color, tubes of what Jack assumed were foundation, some brushes, and one foam head, but that was about as glamorous as it got.

The aroma of cinnamon hanging in the air struck him as odd. Not exactly a staple smell for the backroom of a club he would have thought. He'd imagined it would have been more musky. Jack looked around and saw a scent diffuser plugged into a socket right next to the makeup station.

Sheila leaned against the wall to Jack's left, drumming her false nails against a nail file Jack hadn't even seen her pick up. She studied him a moment, seemingly taking in every inch of his appearance. When their eyes met, she smiled again and tilted her head to the side. Jack found himself inspecting her wig. At least, it seemed like a wig. The blonde hair could have easily been coming out of her own scalp. He didn't see a line or an imperfection anywhere.

"It's called lace-front, honey," Sheila said. "Designed specially to make it look like I grew this all on my own."

Jack's face flooded with heat. "I'm sorry," he said. "I didn't mean to stare." God, could he be any more of a creep?

"It's fine." She pushed herself off the wall and strode over to the mirror, where she took a seat and regarded him again. "People have been watching me all my life. May as well give them something to look at, right?" Jack nodded. But he still felt like a boob. "So what's your style?"

"My . . . my style?"

"Yeah. Which corner of drag calls to you the most? Are you one of the pageant girls? Comedy? Are you a dancer? A singer? Or are you interested in the scandalous underbelly?"

"I . . . um . . ."

After a moment, Sheila sighed. "Let's cut the crap, what do you say?" Her voice had dropped an octave or so, and now it sounded familiar. He just couldn't place where he'd heard it. "It's obvious you don't know enough about drag to care about doing it, so why are you really here?"

Jack bit his bottom lip. "Honestly?" He scratched the back of his head and sighed. "I wanted to talk to you."

"So why didn't you say that? You didn't have to make up a story."

Jack shrugged and leaned against the door. "I don't know. I got nervous and it just came out."

"I hope that doesn't happen often," Sheila said without missing a beat.

Jack blinked. "That sounded dirty."

Sheila tucked a strand of hair behind her ear and turned to the mirror. "Maybe it was." She wiped a smudge of lipstick from the side of her mouth. "Or maybe it wasn't. That, my dear, is for you to decide."

This was his chance. That had basically been an invitation, right? But Jack's legs had turned to lead. He tried to take a step forward, but the only thing he managed to do was stand there and look like a dummy.

Sheila studied him through the mirror and shook her head. "You really are bad at this, aren't you?" She turned back around, spread her legs far enough to run a finger up her inner thigh. "I assume this is what you wanted?"

Jack's mouth went dry. He opened it, but couldn't make a word come out, so closed it again. He simply nodded.

"That's all you had to say, then," Sheila said with a seductive glint in her eyes. "Get your sexy ass over here."

Jack's stomach knotted as he took one step forward. Then another. And another. When he was in arm's reach, Sheila tugged him closer. She slid down his sweats and appraised his dick through his boxer-briefs.

"I've always admired a man who can pull off canary." She sank to her knees and slid the underwear down, and thank God he was still hard. He usually would have lost it by now.

Her face faltered. He didn't have the biggest cock in the world, only average by the American standard, but he hoped it wouldn't stop her from going through with this.

She wrapped her hand around it, looked up at him, and smiled. "This should be fun."

She started forward, but hesitated, eyes closed. Jack's breath hitched. What was happening? Why had she stopped? He needed her to keep going, before he completely lost his nerve.

She stood up and put a few feet between them. "I can't do this," she said, sighing. "Not like this." She looked Jack dead in the eye, and he thought he saw something beneath the lust in her gaze. If he didn't know any better, he would have sworn it was terror. "There's something you should know," she said, reaching for the wig.

Jack practically shouted, "No!" She paused, face a mask of confusion. "I don't want to know. I don't care who you are underneath all that. I just need this right now and I want it to be you. The you that's right here right now." If she pulled that hair off her head, it was over. He'd lose his hard-on and he'd never get it back, and he couldn't have that. Not when he was so close to what he'd wanted for so long.

Sheila studied him a moment longer, then shook her head. "You're sure?"

"Positive."

She raised an eyebrow and watched him for a few seconds before she closed the space between them again. Back on her knees, she looked up at him once more. Finally she dragged her tongue from the base to the tip, taking the head into her mouth and sampling it, then going further. Holy fucking shit his erection was still fully there. Throbbing even. She stroked him at the same time, and he grabbed her head, not to control her but he needed something to hold on to; if he reached for the edge of the table behind her, he'd topple over. It had been far too long since anyone had been down there, let alone anyone he was actually attracted to.

He tangled his fingers in her hair and fuck him sideways it felt real. He'd been with enough women to know the difference between the human and the synthetic. He couldn't put his finger on why, but it turned him on even more that Sheila had spent the extra to complete her illusion. The head of his dick brushed the back of her throat and his knees buckled, but she wrapped her arm around his waist without missing a beat and dragged him closer. Deeper. She gagged, and that one sound almost did him in. The idea that someone was choosing him over oxygen was pretty much the sexiest thing in the world.

He pulled back as much as her guardrail of a forearm would allow, then pushed forward. She murmured her approval around him and he did it again. And again. A moment later he was fucking her face.

Fuck yes. I'm still hard. I can't waste this.

"Please," he panted. "Please let me fuck you."

"Uh-uh, sugar," Sheila said after letting him slide from between her lips with a satisfying *pop*. She wiped a tear from the corner of her eye. "I need more aggression than that. Consent is the bee's knees, and all that, but I like to play a little darker." She kissed the tip, left more of her smeared lipstick there. "Make me feel like I don't have any control." The shaft. "Like you're one of those big, strong, stupid men and you're just going to take what you want, even if I don't like it." His abs. "You think you can do that for me?"

"That sounds like—"

"I didn't say rape me. I just like it really rough. Call it consensual nonconsent. You have my full consent. I just don't want to be in control for a little while. Is that okay with you?"

He wanted to, if only because she might not let him fuck her any other way. But what if she said stop? He'd do it and then she'd get mad and he'd have fucked everything up. How was he supposed to know the difference between a real no and a pretend one?

She brought their lips together and, when she slipped her tongue into his mouth, he could taste himself. "My safeword," she said when she broke away, "is 'rhythm nation.'"

"I don't know what that is . . ." Jack said, then kissed her again and ground his cock against her thigh.

"If it gets to be too much for me. That's how you'll know you've gone too far. I'll say 'rhythm nation.' Other than that, you keep going until we come. Spank me. Humiliate me. Pull my hair. But if you snatch my wig off, I'll kick your ass."

Jack nodded. He understood, now. "Okay. I'm in."

Sheila flashed him her pearly whites. "Great. Give me a second." She removed her tights and panties before squatting and reaching beneath the front of her dress with one hand and down the back of it with the other. Jack heard something ripping away from skin, and Sheila winced. A few seconds later she stood up straight, balling up a length of duct tape; she breathed a sigh of apparent relief. "Tucking is a bitch. And anyone who tells you otherwise is a lying sack." She tossed the trash into the bin next to her bag. "Now let's get this party started, shall we?"

Jack slipped the condom from his pocket, tore it open with his teeth. He wanted to tell Sheila to put it on for him so he could get to full mast again—the untucking had made him slightly uncomfortable—but that probably wouldn't fit the particular fantasy she had in mind. So he stared at her lips, tried to imagine his dick between them again. But it didn't work. He was losing steam and fast.

"Turn around," he grunted.

"Why don't you turn me around?"

He imagined anger flaring inside him, lapping at the underside of his skin and making him sweat. He dropped the rubber on the table, spun Sheila around, and forced her forward. "Don't fucking play with me," he growled, hoping he wasn't taking this too far. "When I tell you to do something, just fucking do it!"

"Okay!" Sheila whimpered. "I'm sorry!"

He lifted her dress above her hips and holy shit that was a nice ass. Plump. Round. She clearly did her squats.

Jack slapped it, first with his hand and then with his cock. Sheila shivered beneath him, and part of him wanted to ask if she was okay, but another, darker part, wanted to make this experience as real as possible for her. "You're so fucking dirty," he said. "Flaunting yourself around like that, teasing me. Teasing all of us. You wanted this from the minute I walked in the club, didn't you?"

"No! I swear! I'm sorry, I didn't mean to—"

"Shut up! I didn't tell you to talk, bitch." She shuddered and fell silent immediately. He must be on the right track. "And then those songs you were dancing to? This shit here?" He yanked at the sequins she wore. "You asked for this." He put his dick between her ass cheeks, humped a few times.

"Please," Sheila whispered. "I don't want this. I'm sorry for whatever I did."

He pulled back and brought his palm down as hard as he could. The fiery imprint it left stared up at him as Sheila sobbed. Maybe she was faking. Maybe she wasn't. That didn't matter. The only thing that mattered was that she have a good time. He grabbed the condom. He still wasn't totally hard again, but the erection was manageable. More than he would have had any of the times before.

He rolled it down himself and spat on Sheila's hole. He'd forgotten his lube at home and was afraid that asking her if she had any would ruin her illusion. He smeared his saliva against her taint and pressed inside.

He had to fight to keep his balance. She was tight. Tighter than anywhere he'd ever been, and fuck all if he wasn't already trying to figure out how to control himself.

"Please!" Sheila cried. "Please, I'm sorry! Stop!"

But that wasn't the word. So he kept going. Grabbed her shoulders and fucked her like she'd stolen from him. It was working. He was completely erect again, and even though the fact that Sheila was really a man niggled at the back of his mind, it didn't matter. He looked in the mirror and saw her hair falling around her face in curtains. Every thrust sent another shock wave, and her face was scrunched up, lips pulled away from clenched teeth. But then their eyes met and she gave him a small nod.

"Don't fucking look at me," he barked. Her walls constricted around him, and he grabbed a handful of her hair and held on. He wanted to yank, to see how strong the hold was, but he didn't dare have the wig come off in his hand and scar him for the rest of his life. He was close anyway. So he wrapped his other hand around her throat, and that was clearly all she needed. Her eyes rolled back in her head, her body convulsed, and suddenly she was mumbling incoherently, shuddering from head to toe. He let her go and she fell forward. Jack slowed his strokes, but she met him, throwing her ass back and dancing on him. The visual of her cheeks engulfing him like that was too much to handle and he shot his load.

He couldn't keep his eyes open so he closed them, pressed in as deep as he could go, and rode the wave.

When he could breathe again, he pulled out and promptly tumbled to the ground. He panted. Sheila turned around and knelt between his legs, dabbing at his face with a towel she must have grabbed from her makeup kit.

"That was amazing," she said. "Thank you." She slipped the condom off him and tossed it into the bin. "Let me see your phone." He obeyed without even thinking about it. "That's my number," she said after punching a few buttons. "We should do this again sometime."

Jack grunted his agreement. He heard the chair slide by the mirror and from the corner of his eye saw Sheila sit down gingerly. After a moment, he had enough strength to climb to his feet, clean himself off the rest of the way, and pull his pants back up. "Thanks." He didn't know what to say, so he turned around and let himself out of the dressing room.

He'd just fucked a guy. Damn near thirty years old and he'd actually lost his dude virginity. It was a dream come fucking true. Maybe now he could *really* be himself. Maybe he could find a woman who was okay with him being bi. Or a man, even. Maybe the universe was finally smiling on him.

Or maybe it was setting him up for the biggest fuck you of all.

CHAPTER TWO

Ryan shuffled through the papers on his desk, searching for the Benning case file for the twelfth time, but still no luck. Hopefully Christie had made copies. A knock on the door gave him pause, finger hovering over the intercom button.

"Come in," he said.

When Jack walked in, Ryan almost fell over. Jack stood in the doorway, suit pressed and hair gelled up, flashing that Welcome-to-Jack's-place-I'll-be-glad-to-fuck-you-now smile. "Morning, boss."

His shoulders seemed broader this morning and God, that jacket fit so well to his body it seemed to be made specifically for him. His eyes sparkled; they stood out more than usual because of his silver tie. The man knew how to accentuate his features. Ryan flashed back to the way Jack's hard-on had pressed against the fabric of his sweatpants and sat down before something popped up he didn't feel like explaining. He pretended to search for a file on his desk so he didn't seem to be staring. "Good morning."

After a few seconds, Ryan glanced back up at him. Did he know that they'd hooked up last night? That he'd had Ryan practically begging for his cock? What if he did? Ryan's pulse quickened at the thought.

"You look like you're in a good mood this morning," Ryan said, clearing his throat.

"Do I?" The smug bastard. Did Jack know the truth? Was that why he seemed so happy? Maybe he was about to bend him over the desk and show him a repeat performance. But then Ryan remembered that he'd been getting ready to reveal himself last night, and Jack had nearly jumped out of his skin trying to stop him.

Ryan readjusted himself under the desk. He needed to be professional. This was a place of business, after all. "Yeah. You do." He scanned Jack's face for a sign of anything else. Any inkling that his secret was out and that he should be at home packing so he could run for the hills. He suddenly regretted giving Jack the number of the texting app he'd downloaded. Sure, he could delete it, but Jack wasn't the only one with the number. Other queens at the club, promoters, and club management had it too. It was how he kept his professional day and professional night life separate.

Jack shrugged, but never lost that grin. "I'm finished going over this, so I figured I'd bring it back."

Ryan zeroed in on the folder in Jack's hand. *There* was the fucking file. "I've been looking for that everywhere. I thought I'd lost my mind."

Jack set it on top of Ryan's in-box and hovered there for a moment.

"Was there something else I could help you with?" Ryan swallowed, bracing himself for the bombshell.

Jack opened his mouth, but said nothing. Now that he was standing so close, it was clear that something wasn't right. He still looked downright jovial on the surface, but there was pain there too. Maybe Ryan hadn't noticed it at first, but Jack's smile suddenly seemed fake, and it didn't quite reach his eyes. He appeared . . . tormented.

After nearly a full minute, Ryan said, "Are you okay?"

Jack's mouth snapped shut, and he shook his head as though shaking a thought away. "Yeah. Yeah, I'm fine, sorry. Just . . . zoned out for a second there."

"You sure?"

Jack nodded. "I was thinking about something that happened last night, but . . ."

Ryan's heart plummeted into his feet. Fuck. Jack *did* know. What was he going to do?

"I, uh, I'm gonna get back to work. I've got some more research to do before we go to trial."

Ryan drew a breath. Timid relief spread through him. "Okay," he said, trying to mask the shakiness of his voice. "Would you shut the door on your way out, please?"

"Sure thing." Jack licked his lips, his tongue sliding first across the top and then dragging the bottom slightly into his mouth. Ryan thought he might pass out. Jack turned to leave.

He paused with his hand on the knob. Maybe he wanted to say something else. Or talk about something. But before Ryan could question him, Jack shook his head once again and was gone.

That was unusual. Jack was the poster boy for workplace professionalism. Always on time, never talked back when it wasn't necessary, never zoned out. On one hand, Ryan wanted to find out what was bothering him. He knew people thought he was heartless, and that was how he needed them to think. He had a law firm to run, and he and the other partners had reputations to uphold. But really he was a great big softy inside and cared deeply for most everyone that worked for him. On the other hand, it wasn't like he and Jack were friends. Sure, they'd fucked last night, but that didn't mean they were close now. Jack obviously didn't know he'd been banging his boss. It would be strange for Ryan to suddenly start chatting him up and taking an interest in his personal life. Right?

Ryan pushed the thought from his mind. If Jack wanted to talk about whatever was bothering him, he would. If not, it was none of Ryan's business.

He paged through the case file. Stephanie Benning had a good case for workplace discrimination. She was suing her former employer for wrongful termination. Her boss hadn't been too happy when Stephen began showing up as Stephanie, and had been pretty vocal about it until he'd fired her. At first, Ryan had thought the case would be open and shut, but then the company's lawyers had cried about religious freedoms, and now things were getting ugly. Ryan had brought Jack on to second chair, but he might need more help than that. They still had a few weeks until they went to court, so he had a little bit of time, but not much.

They were going to do their best to stick it to that asshole.

He wondered if his own colleagues would act like Mr. Pompeo if they found out about Ryan's alter ego, though. Someone who had worked for him for sixteen years had one day shown up to work, announcing that she was no longer the person they'd known her as; drag wasn't the same as being trans, but many people related the two.

The other partners' reactions, not to mention Jack's, would probably be similar if it ever got out that Ryan Swift spent five nights a week at Neon Trees as Sheila Saltue. There'd be shock, of course. Maybe even some backlash. But nothing to the extent of termination.

Ryan wondered—as he'd done more and more often lately—if he should just come out and let everyone know the truth. Honestly, what was the worst they could do?

You let an associate fuck you like a dirty little bitch boy, his mind supplied. *Told him to do terrible things to you and you fucking loved it.* Ryan took a deep breath. That part definitely couldn't get out. Not ever. And it could never happen again. *Not to mention the fact that clients would leave the firm in droves. People don't want to be represented by a* drag queen, *now do they?* Right again. Drag still wasn't all the way accepted, and he couldn't risk what he'd worked so hard to build. So he would keep under the covers. No one needed to know.

Especially not Jack. Even though it had been some pretty spectacular sex. It was absolutely a one-time thing. It didn't matter that he could still feel Jack inside him, or that his ass cheeks burned where Jack had spanked him. Yeah, maybe he had wanted to jump Jack as soon as he came through the door, but Ryan had controlled himself. Because that's what being an adult was all about.

But he was getting hard again. He needed to get out of the office for a bit. Get outside and let the fresh air clear his mind. Grab a bite to eat, maybe. Everything would still be here when he got back. He flipped the folder closed, and pulled his jacket off the stand just inside the door.

The rest of the office was bustling, and he hoped he could get lost in the shuffle and no one would stop him. He did, however, lean down as he passed Christie's desk. "I'm taking an early lunch."

"Alrighty, sir." She smiled and typed something into her computer.

Ryan nodded and continued toward the elevator. This would be exactly what he needed. He hoped. The door slid shut and he was mercifully alone. He punched the button for the bottom floor, then leaned against the wall as the car made its descent.

His phone buzzed. Praying it was just a news alert or email, he fished the phone from his pocket. But it was a text.

From Jack.

He was once again thrilled that he'd given Jack the texting app number so he didn't figure out his true identity.

Heart pounding and head suspiciously light, Ryan opened the message. He wasn't sure if the two words written on the screen made him happy or want to puke. He stared at them until the doors parted and then closed. He shook his head and jabbed the Open button and made a beeline for the front door. This couldn't be happening. But it was. And God help him, he actually found himself considering Jack's request. He looked at it again, but refused to respond yet. He'd get his mind right first, and then send back something thoughtful explaining why it couldn't happen. Or maybe he wouldn't. Ugh! This shouldn't be so difficult. He shouldn't be having this debate with himself because it was absolutely out of the question. He'd already established that. His body had other ideas, though. He read Jack's text one more time.

Wanna meet?

Ryan *did* want to meet. And more. He'd known when Jack approached him after the show that he should have turned him away, but watching him get closer, all boyish and nervous . . . Sheila just couldn't bear the thought of disappointing him.

Ryan often thought of Sheila as a separate being. She was everything he wasn't: outgoing, witty, overtly sexual. It was her part of his personality that leaned most heavily toward seeing Jack again.

But it would be a terrible mistake. Especially if Jack found out the truth. What if he already had? Could that be what this was about? No . . . he couldn't possibly know already. If he had, he would have mentioned it earlier, right?

Ryan's phone dinged. He eyed it warily. It was facedown on his desk, so if he just left it like that, he wouldn't have to read the message at all. But curiosity got the better of him and he picked it up.

Sorry. I forgot how you like things. You're going to meet me behind the club tonight. Make sure you're wearing your shortest skirt and no underwear. I'm going to fuck you against that wall where anyone who walks by can see. Be there by 7:30. If you're even a minute late, you get nothing.

Ryan swallowed. He adjusted himself through his pants, resisting the urge to jerk off right there in his office. He typed out a quick *I'll be there* and dropped the device in his drawer. Fuck, he needed to focus. He closed his eyes, took several deep breaths, counting to ten after each one.

Ryan didn't know why he liked having no control so much. He hadn't realized how it turned him on until college, and ever since then, he'd sought out guys who could fulfill that part of him, but none of them had ever seemed to get that into it.

Jack seemed to have promise, though. Ryan didn't allow himself the hope that Jack might be the true top to his bottom, but hell, they could sure have fun trying to figure it out, right?

Once he got his brain under control again, he finished drafting the opening argument for the trial he had the following morning, and headed out. He was cutting it kinda close on time, though. It would take him at least half an hour to make it home in the rush-hour traffic, and then another hour to get showered and into drag. It would be dark, so he probably didn't need to go full glam, but he'd still need to apply a layer of foundation and some lipstick, at minimum.

He called for a car and, by the time he got outside, it was already waiting. He climbed in, gave the driver his address, and they were off.

There was a nasty accident on the interstate, so it took him almost forty-five minutes to get home. He tipped the driver, then dashed inside, peeling off his suit as soon as he was through the door. By the time he made it up to his bedroom, his belt was off and he stripped down the rest of the way. The faint aroma of gardenias in the air made him pause, eyeing the room suspiciously. His jewelry box was closer to the edge of the dresser than he'd left it. There wasn't time to look around to see what else was out of place, but it told him the cleaning service had been by.

Fresh towels had been laid out in the bathroom, and the porcelain sparkled like a diamond in the sunlight. He appreciated the cleaning, he really did. It was just off-putting sometimes to come home and find things different than how he'd left them. But he didn't have time to focus on that, so he showered, shaved, and was back out in record time.

He wasn't a fan of day drag, but it was getting dark enough that he should be able to pull it off without anyone clocking him as a man in a dress. He pulled a tight little black miniskirt from Sheila's closet and held it out for inspection. He'd probably need to slather himself in oil to get in it and use the jaws of life to get out of it, but it was the shortest one he owned. So he laid it across the bed and paired it with a bright-pink halter top. Next was hair. On the one hand, it might be better to go with something short; that would work best with the outfit, especially since he wasn't padding. But Jack seemed to like the longer wig he'd worn last night. If he went with that option, though, he'd need to make sure it was pinned down extra tight, because Jack had nearly yanked the last one off his head.

In the end, Ryan selected a red bob-cut lace-front. The back came halfway down his neck, so it was a nice combination of coverage and just enough for Jack to grab a fistful of. They said that gentlemen preferred blondes, but it wasn't the gentleman Ryan was hoping to bring out tonight, and this wig, paired with that outfit, said, *Fuck me stupid*, better than he ever could.

He put on his makeup in record time, not bothering to contour or add an excessive amount of detail; only one person would be watching him tonight, and Jack probably wouldn't care how pretty Sheila's face was when it was pressed against a brick wall. Ryan added a layer of powder to set the foundation, clipped his wig into place, and got dressed. Fitting into that skirt was indeed a chore that took far longer than it should have, but once the whole look was put together, even he had to admit that he'd fuck himself. Ordinarily, he didn't like wearing the nude lip color, but it worked tonight. He gave his head a quick, but vigorous shake to make sure the wig wouldn't budge, and once he was satisfied, checked himself out in the mirror. The reflection was basic, but it was Sheila. And Sheila was beautiful. She blew herself a kiss and headed out.

The sun had dipped below the horizon by the time she got outside, and dusk was starting to give way to twilight. It should be safe enough to walk, by now. The club was only a few blocks away, and she still had thirty minutes before she was supposed to meet Jack.

Surprisingly, she only met a few people on her trip there, the scariest of whom was a man with a skinned head and tattoos of skulls on his face and a Support Trump button on his collar. Sweat ran down the back of her neck, and she wished she'd brought her purse out with her. There was a pair of brass knuckles in case she ever needed them. Her heels were only four inches, and she prepared to make a run for it if she needed to. But the man only tipped his head in Sheila's direction and kept on about his business. She sighed, her heart beating a mile a minute.

The air felt different tonight. Normally, she walked this same route and everything was fine, but tonight unease crept its way down her spine, prickling her flesh. Sheila wasn't the type to walk with her head down, but she found herself not wanting to make eye contact with anyone. Even now that full dark had spread across the sky, she still felt . . . off.

Paranoia caressed her, and she spared a glance behind her to make sure she wasn't being followed. When she turned back around, she collided with someone. Sheila grunted in surprise, then said, "I'm so sorry!"

He wore a baseball cap pulled low and an upturned collar. "Don't worry about it." He kept walking. She hadn't gotten a look at his face, but she knew that voice. From where, though, she couldn't place. Her emotions were too heightened; she wasn't sure she'd recognize her own voice at this point. She shook off the nerves and kept going, glancing over her shoulder every few steps. The nerves crept back. Who was that guy? And why had he made the hairs on her arms stand on end. Something wasn't right, but she didn't have time to try to figure it out. She just hoped she'd never see him again.

When she made it to the club, she had fifteen minutes to spare.

She debated going in for a drink, but decided against it. There probably wouldn't be enough time to finish it before Jack got there, and then it would lay abandoned on the ground while she got the stuffing fucked out of her, then stay forgotten until some rat or something carried it away. She dipped into the alley and leaned against the wall.

It took an eternity for Jack to get there. Every person that walked by, she hoped was him, only to be disappointed. She couldn't remember being this excited about anything—or anyone—in ages. Mainly because she never got excited anymore unless she was performing. That was the way she liked it. Because when she got happy, she let her guard down. And when she let it down, she let herself get too reeled in. That was how hearts got broken.

Jack strolled into the alley about ten minutes later, looking all sexy and full of charm and totally different than how he'd appeared in the office earlier, though he was still in his suit and tie. Sheila swallowed and bit her bottom lip. Were those super-nerves? Armored butterflies? *Get it together*, she told herself.

"Wow," Jack said, and his baritone washed over her like warm honey. "You follow instructions well."

"I was always taught following instructions was part of life."

Jack took a step forward. "That's good advice."

Sheila's breath hitched. He was right in front of her, now. Whatever he'd used in the shower smelled amazing, and she found herself getting drunk on the scent. And then he kissed her. Full. Deep. She melted into him. His hands gripped her shoulders, pulled her up so they were on more even ground. Sheila wasn't that much shorter than Jack, especially in these heels, but it still impressed her that he could lift her so easily. Their embrace became darker, more aggressive. Jack shoved her against the wall. In less than a heartbeat he was on her, first simply breathing against her lips. Then he crushed their mouths together again. She heard him struggling with his belt and broke their kiss. She wanted to see his dick spring out the same way it had last night. He was grinning when she next looked up.

"This what you want?" he breathed. He didn't bother undoing his pants, just unzipped them and pulled his cock out. It bobbed expectantly, and she dropped to her knees without hesitation. "Ah, ah," he said, gripping her chin forcefully. "Did I tell you that you could suck me?"

Sheila swallowed. She stared at him, torn between her lust and desire to obey. He watched her for what felt like a millennium before pushing his hips forward, brushing her lips with the head of his dick. She started to open her mouth, but he raised an eyebrow and she paused. His scent wafted toward her. God, he smelled so manly and she fucking loved it. It was like he'd been on the move and running all day. There was sweat mixed in with the earthy undertones of soap and the faintest trace of the lube he'd probably used to masturbate earlier. Sheila wasn't sure what she wanted more: the gratification that was sure to come from tasting him again, or the punishment she hoped he'd be able to dole out for disobeying.

She stayed perfectly still for a minute, perhaps longer. Cars zoomed by on the street beyond, and the barest whiff of urine tickled her senses, but those were the only indications that there was a world beyond the two of them.

Jack caressed Sheila's hair, and she racked her brain trying to remember if she'd been forbidden to move or just to suck. It seemed like an admiring touch, a reward for doing as she'd been told, and she wanted to lean into it, cherish it. But she decided to play it safe and not move at all.

They continued watching each other, and finally, after what felt like a decade, the side of Jack's mouth tilted up in a smile and he gave an almost imperceptible nod. She licked her lips. She wanted to attack his cock; go at it with everything she had and not stop until he was a shivering mess on the ground. But she was a lady, damn it. So instead she dragged her tongue leisurely across the tip, letting the tang wash over her taste buds.

She teased him slowly, sensually, tracing every inch of his shaft. Part of her wanted him to take control already, but she was content driving him to the brink of madness until he was ready. Sucking one ball into her mouth, she rolled it around before switching to the other; his soft moans told her that he was enjoying it. She wanted— no *needed* more. She moved back up and deep-throated him in one swoop. He groaned loudly and tried to press himself deeper. There was the magic. But it still wasn't quite enough. She tugged at his nuts, massaging them with her hand while her tongue worked him. He stumbled forward, and then there was nothing between her head and the wall and he pulled out, slid back in slowly. Again. And again. Each time, he got a little harder, until he was fucking her face and there was nowhere she could run, even if she wanted to. Every thrust drove her against the bricks.

Just how she liked it. No respect. Not thinking of her comfort at all.

She opened her mouth further, tried to breathe in between strokes because she couldn't do it through her nose at all.

"Close it!" he barked, and she did so without another thought. "Oh, that's it," he murmured. He slowed down just enough for her to catch her breath, and she was grateful, but wanted him to take it to the next level now. She couldn't ask, though, so how could she signal him that she was ready?

She reached around, cupped his ass and squeezed, but he didn't seem to get the message, so she slapped it. After several attempts, Jack still acted completely oblivious, so she pushed him away.

"I have to go," she said, wiping her mouth and standing up. She had no intention of leaving right now—she'd never be able to hide the hard-on in a skirt this tight—but if this didn't clue him in that she was ready to get fucked, nothing would. "Thanks for a great time, sugar." She headed for the street.

She felt his eyes on her as she made it ten feet away. Fifteen. Twenty. She sighed. Maybe he wasn't the guy she'd thought he was, after all. She knew it was weird, but she didn't want to have to actually say that she was ready for him to be inside her. He was supposed to just know.

She was about to step out of the alley when his hand closed around her mouth and he yanked her back.

"I don't remember saying you could go anywhere."

There it was. She flooded her basement as he slammed her against the wall. Fuck it hurt, but come morning she would rub the sore spots and wish he'd done it a little harder.

"Who the fuck do you think you are?"

"I'm sorry," she mumbled against his palm.

"You still haven't learned your lesson, have you? Strutting around and teasing me with that pretty mouth of yours? And this ass?" He slapped it for emphasis. "Tell me it's mine."

Desire curled in her stomach. Holy shit, he was good at this. "No. It's mine," she said when he pulled his hand away. "Now please, let me go."

He struck her ass again, held his hand there, and dug into the flesh with his nails. The pain was intense at first, but then her eyes nearly rolled back as it gave way to ecstasy. She hadn't felt pain this good in she-couldn't-remember-how-long.

"Please," she sobbed. Tears actually blurred her vision as she struggled to try to crane her neck to face Jack, but his forearm pressed her against the wall and she was all but immobilized. "I promise I won't tell anyone. Just . . . just let me leave."

"Oh, I know you won't." He lifted her skirt, dragged a finger along her ass before pressing it against her taint. "You don't really want to leave me, do you?"

"Yes," she whispered. She didn't trust her voice to go any higher because it might crack and betray how bad she wanted him.

"Really?" He dipped that finger inside and holy fuck it *burned*. Sheila bit her lower lip to keep from screaming. As long as she'd been having sex, she'd never thought to tell them to do it without lubrication. She filed that away for future use. He added another, and it was all she could do not to push back, ride those fingers until he was ready to give her the real thing.

But he was apparently content teasing her for now, because he fucked her with his fingers, hard and fast. He curled one, and she wondered if he was searching for her spot. She mumbled something—even she couldn't tell what it was. Nothing mattered as long as he didn't ever stop. After a minute or so, he did, and it took everything she had not to turn on him and lose her mind.

"Don't fucking move," he growled as though he'd read her mind.

So she stayed there, frozen in place while he tore the condom open and rolled it down himself. One hand grabbed the back of her neck, keeping her face pressed against the wall, while the other gripped her waist and pulled her to him. "Don't you move."

"Please. Don't do this."

"Shut up. You're getting what you deserve, you little cocktease."

She didn't mean to moan so loudly. It just came out. No man had ever been so forceful, so dirty with her and kept it up this long. They were usually bitching by this point how it was too weird and they couldn't take it. But she would. She would take everything he had to give her and more. Because she was dirty and she needed to be punished.

Jack spat on her hole, smeared it with the head of his dick, and then sank in with no warning. She bit the inside of her cheek, but not before she let out a strangled cry. Surely someone had heard that. They could come bursting in at any moment and call the cops and then Sheila would be forced into an awkward position where she'd have to explain to the police that no she wasn't being raped, she was only pretending like she was. That was if they didn't beat the shit out of her for being a drag queen in the first place.

But no one came. There were no running footsteps. No shouts of "What are you doing to her!" No flashlights being shined in their face. Nothing but Jack fucking her brains out all over that wall.

"Stop . . . it . . . please . . ." She could barely get the words out, and he definitely wasn't slowing down. In fact, with every protest, he got more passionate, more aggressive. Suddenly his hand was wrapped around her throat, bending her toward him as he nailed her. He grabbed a fistful of hair and wrenched her head to the side, exposing her neck, then he sunk his teeth into the flesh there. White-hot pain exploded, and the myriad of sensations was too much. She blew her load against the front of her skirt. Her body seized as stars exploded behind her eyelids and she tried to keep her eyes from rolling all the way back. Her skin was hot and her legs had turned to Jell-O. She was glad she had the wall to support her. She wanted to ride the wave as long as she possibly could. She must have gripped him extra tight, because he grunted and said, "Oh here it comes, bitch. I'm about to come all in that ass." Her own jizz was sticking her skirt to her leg at this point, but she did as much as she could to help him along. Squeezed a little tighter, twerked as much as his death grip on her waist would allow. "Oh . . . my . . . gaaah!"

His entire body went rigid, but he didn't stop thrusting. It felt awkward. She wouldn't complain, though, because she'd never been fucked like that before. He collapsed against her back, panting. She wasn't sure how long they stayed that way before he pulled out.

After a few seconds, Sheila mustered enough strength to turn around and look him in the eye. His face was that of a wild man. Eyes crazed, hair matted to his skin with sweat, face red and blotchy. Great. A job well done. Already she found herself wishing they didn't have to separate. That she could take him back to her house with her and they could fuck like horny teenagers all night. But then how would she keep him from discovering who she really was?

Reality set in. She couldn't let him know. Firstly, because she couldn't be a named partner in a law firm fucking an associate. Secondly, because what proof did she have that he wouldn't spill her secret to everyone else? If that happened, her career would be over. So no. This couldn't ever happen again. No matter how badly she wanted it to.

"I . . . I have to go."

She tried to get around him, but he stopped her. "Hold on a sec." He kissed her again. Slower this time. He seemed to put more of himself into the kiss, and it was all she could do not to pledge her undying devotion. But that wasn't her thinking. That was her hormones and the dark part of herself that craved pain and degradation. The part she had to keep under control. So she did what any other self-respecting woman would do, copped a feel and broke the kiss.

"Thanks for a great time, big guy." And she left before he could say anything else.

She headed for the street as quickly as she could, adjusting her skirt on the way. Part of her wanted to make it out onto the sidewalk this time without him snatching her back, and wasn't sure if she was grateful or disappointed when she did. It didn't matter. When she got home, she'd delete his number, maybe even block him so she wasn't tempted to go there a third time.

She knew herself, though. None of that would work once her body started talking to her again. She'd cave. And she'd call him. Or he'd text her. She was a sucker for a pretty face, and now that they'd fucked—she didn't dare think of what they'd done being graceful enough to be called sleeping together—she was hooked. That was how she'd ended up in that alley. Once she got a taste of anything she wanted, she could be strong until opportunity presented itself, and then she might as well be an addict. Relapse, party of one. But maybe they'd be able to keep it casual. They could keep it professional in the workplace and filthy in the bedroom. How often did that work?

And was she ready to take that chance yet?

INTERLUDE UNKNOWN

I stood in the shadows, ball cap pulled low over my eyes, and watched. There was a club across the street with a large *Neon Trees* sign above the door. Men and women came and went, most of them greeting each other like old friends. Cars zoomed up and down the street, creating a convenient buffer. Perhaps it was a gay club; a lot of the guys that came out of there had more than a little sissy in their walks. I could see that from here.

The cars slowed to a halt as the light at the end of the block went from yellow to red. I shrank back against the wall, praying that I was hidden. The majority of people most likely wouldn't be able to see me, but all I needed was one, and then I'd be answering a million questions I wasn't in the mood for. I pulled my coat a little higher on my shoulders.

Traffic started moving again and I got a nose-full of exhaust. I shook my head, resisting the urge to cough.

Didn't look like there was anyone here. Not anyone who really called to me, anyway. But finding someone shouldn't have been so . . . time-consuming. With a sigh, I waited for the light to turn once more, and started across the road. If there was one thing I liked about Sapphire Bay, it was the robust nightlife. People always out and about meant the night was always rife with potential victims.

I stepped onto the sidewalk, and the music from inside the club drifted out at me as the door snapped shut while the bouncer inspected the next person. I walked right past. I didn't know where I was heading, but damn it, I needed to figure it out fast or I'd be getting on the train back home empty-handed.

But right at that moment, a suspiciously large woman brushed past me and stepped into the alley a few yards ahead. I paused for half a second before following her into the darkness.

I had to let her know how dangerous that was.

CHAPTER THREE

Jack found himself in front of the mirror, running his fingers through his hair. He couldn't remember the last time he'd cared how he looked for someone, but Sheila was obviously putting so much energy into her appearance, it would be disrespectful to meet her like he just rolled out of bed.

He had seen Sheila every night for nearly two weeks. Most nights they fucked, but every once in a while, they managed actual conversation. Nothing too deep, but they were getting to know each other.

The clock on his nightstand told him he had about half an hour before Sheila got there, so he let his towel drop and went straight for the closet.

He pulled a mint-green button-up on along with a pair of designer underwear and jeans. He debated ordering food, but he never knew where the night would take them. They'd probably stay in the whole time, but there was always that air of unpredictability with her. She was a woman—*man!*—who liked to have fun. The other night had consisted of going out to the wharf and making fun of the guys with muscles bigger than their heads.

"There's sexy," she'd said, caressing Jack's biceps, "and then there's 'roid rage waiting to happen."

Well, they'd need to eat, whatever they did, right? So he'd order in and they'd go from there. Now he wondered if he should change into a tighter shirt. Give her something to look at. Five minutes later he hung up with the China Hut and plopped down on the couch. He glanced at his watch. She'd be arriving any minute, and fuck if his heart wasn't running a marathon now. He needed to calm himself down. Everything was fine.

He flipped on the television.

The woman on screen had her blonde hair tied up in a bun and a thick-framed pair of glasses sitting high on her nose.

"Details of the grizzly slaying are still rolling in," the newswoman said. She shifted, plucking briefly at the buttons of her blazer. "The victim's identity is being withheld by police, but a source has revealed that he went by the stage name Valentine Heartbreak, a drag performer at the Neon Trees nightclub."

What the hell? Jack sat a little straighter, turned the volume higher, but it felt wrong, somehow. She reminded him of those librarians he'd always see in TV shows that patrolled the stacks, silencing anyone who spoke above a thought.

"The performer was found in a dumpster behind his apartment building, stripped naked with his throat slashed. Police do not believe robbery was a motive. More on this story as it develops." Jack saw a hint of disgust on her face. But he wasn't sure if it was because of the murder or because the victim was a drag queen. What she thought of it didn't matter.

Did Sheila know the slain queen? Were they friends? Did she even know?

A knock on the door snapped Jack back to reality. He got up, smoothed his shirt down, and let Sheila inside. She greeted him with a kiss that he only returned halfheartedly.

"Is everything okay?" she asked, concern and maybe a trace of fear marring her features.

"Um, yeah," Jack said. "Kinda. I think. Here, come sit down with me." He jerked his head in the direction of the sofa and Sheila followed. When they were both sitting, he took a moment to collect himself. He wasn't sure why this had shaken him so much. He didn't even know this Valentine person. But he knew Sheila. And he actually cared for her. So maybe this one hit a little too close to home.

He took a deep breath. "How many of the other girls did you know at the club?"

Sheila shrugged. "All of them, for the most part, except this one little Barbie girl who started a few weeks ago." She smiled warmly.

"We're all a pretty tight-knit family. Us girls gotta stick together, you know?"

Shit. That made this that much harder. Jack's stomach churned. He focused on a patch of cracked paint on the wall across the room that he'd been meaning to get fixed for months. He couldn't look Sheila in the eye right now. Hell, he didn't even really know how to tell her.

"Hey," she said, touching his chin gently and catching his gaze. "What's wrong?"

"Um . . ." He swallowed the lump in his throat. "There was a news report just before you got here. They, uh, they said that police found a man's body in a dumpster a little while ago. And they wouldn't release the man's name, but the anchor said that a source had confirmed that he was one of the girls at Neon Trees."

Sheila's eyes went wide, glassy. Her mouth hung slightly open. "Which one?" she whispered. Her bottom lip trembled as though she was already expecting the worst.

". . . Valentine Heartbreak."

Sheila's expression crumbled. "No," she said, voice breaking. Tears streamed from her eyes. She shook her head slowly. "No. That can't be true. They—they made a mistake. Valentine isn't d— She's not de— Oh God!" She threw her arms around him and buried her face in his shoulder. She bawled as though she'd lost her best friend, and Jack wanted to cry too. It hurt him that she hurt. He hugged her as tight as he could, because there was nothing else he could do, nothing he could say to relieve the pain that she must be feeling.

He couldn't say how long they sat there. It could have been minutes—it could have been hours—but after a while Sheila stood up. "Excuse me," she sobbed, and made a beeline for the bathroom.

Jack touched the wet spot on his shoulder; he hadn't even noticed it when she'd been there, but now it was obvious, and growing colder. He went to his room and changed into a fresh shirt and, by the time he got back, Sheila was sitting on the couch again, dabbing at the sides of her eyes with a balled-up tissue. Jack sat down next to her, put an arm around her.

"We started at the same time. At that same club. We learned together. Grew together, you know?" She sniffled. "I just . . . I don't want to believe she's gone." She took a deep, shaky breath. "His real name was Tim. Tim Branch. He was one of my best friends. One of the greatest men I ever knew." She broke into another fit of sobbing. Jack held her, trying to keep himself from losing it too. He felt useless. Didn't know what to say. What to do. No one close to him had ever been killed.

His parents had tried to sell him that shit about *better places* and *finally being out of pain* when his grandmother had died and he'd hated it then, so he wasn't about to shovel a helping of the same thing in Sheila's direction.

After a few minutes she seemed to regain herself. She cleared her hair—it was brunette, tonight—out of her face. Some of her makeup had smudged; Jack could see a sliver of skin under the layer of foundation, and his heart skipped a beat.

He wasn't sure he was ready to see the person under the persona. It scared—no, *terrified* him that there was a man under all that makeup. If he saw him, that might be the end of their sexual relationship. Jack had a hard enough time keeping his erection with her sometimes as it was. Actually knowing the real man, while ideal in most relationships, could ruin this one.

Jack shook the thoughts away. Maybe all of that was true, but if it was, he would deal with it later. This wasn't the time or the place. Now, the only thing that mattered was consoling Sheila.

"I'm sorry." She blew her nose. "I shouldn't be crying all over you like this. I should go."

"No. Stay. Please." He wiped another tear away with his thumb. "I don't want you out there by yourself." *Especially if this isn't just a random murder*, he didn't add.

"That would be a seriously bad idea," she said, shaking her head.

"Why?"

She stared him dead in the eye. "Because you're not ready to see me without makeup on. And I'm not about to sleep in all this."

"It's fine." *No it's not.* "I can deal." *No, you can't.* "I've been thinking that I want to know what you really look like, anyway." *Stop fucking lying, you fucking liar!*

"Even so . . ." Sheila dropped her gaze and stared off into the distance. "I'm not ready for you to see me."

"Why? What could be so different in and out of drag?"

Sheila chuckled. "Everything, darling. Everything." She got up and headed toward the door.

"Please. I don't want you to go," Jack said. She kept walking. "Sheila, please." She was almost there now and his pulse was racing. "Damn it, Sheila, I said no!"

That stopped her. She turned around, a sad smile on her face. "That only works during sex, sweetheart." And she began to leave again.

Jack was up and across the room before he even knew what he was doing. He snagged her hand and spun her around, ready to press her against the wall. Fuck, that had been the wrong move. Did desperation make people dumb?

He loosened his hold and hovered as nonthreateningly as he could, because the second she changed her mind (*if* she changed her mind), he was going to pull her into the tightest hug he'd ever given anyone. "Then I will fuck you until the sun comes up and both of us have to miss work." Even he didn't believe what he was saying. There was no force in his voice. Just undisguised pleading. He didn't know what else to do. What else to say. If she still resisted, he would let her leave without any more restriction. But he had to try one last time.

Sheila made no effort to move, she simply stood there, watching him and seemingly weighing her options. Jack moved in hesitantly. A soft brush of the lips he wasn't sure was more to calm her nerves or his own. She didn't resist or pull away. Maybe she'd stay, after all.

A knock on the door and he took a step back. Her eyes flitted toward the peephole.

"Who is it?" he asked, crestfallen. She was really going to go. And there wasn't a damn thing he could do to stop it.

"China Hut."

Fuck. He'd completely forgotten he'd ordered for them. "Just a second," he said, putting more distance between them and letting Sheila straighten her dress and hair. He opened the door. "Hey, Tony."

The familiar delivery man greeted him warmly. Jack expected Sheila to squeeze between them and disappear, but she stayed put while he paid, and when he closed the door she was looking down. Jack swallowed. "You're going to stay?"

She glanced up at him, tears standing in her eyes once again. "Promise me you won't think any differently of me if I do."

"Why would I—"

"Just promise me, Jack."

"Fine. I promise." What could be so bad? Was she an extraterrestrial underneath all those cosmetics?

"Okay. Then I'm going to go wash all this off."

She cast one final, almost pleading stare at him and, when he didn't say anything, shuffled off toward the bathroom.

He put the food down on the coffee table in front of the TV and grabbed some plates and glasses from the kitchen. The faucet in the bathroom turned on. He really wasn't ready for this, but it was the only way to keep her from leaving. And he'd made such a big deal of it that it was impossible to back out now. Besides, they couldn't keep this up forever. Sure, their relationship was mostly sex for now, but Jack could easily see it blossoming into something more. Maybe it was the lust talking, but he really cared for her. And you couldn't have a relationship, hell even a friendship, with someone if it was built on lies. It was time to shit or get off the pot.

Jack had almost finished loading the plates with their dinner—a combination of General Tso's chicken, steamed broccoli, fried rice, and a new sampler platter that he'd never tried before—when the water turned off. He straightened up, heart pounding. He was ready for this. He could do it. He was a grown man. He could handle seeing the guy (even though the thought made him a little dizzy) out of drag. As he was.

He felt the floor rumble before he heard the footsteps. He swallowed hard and closed his eyes before he turned around. Everything would be fine. He could do this.

Jack opened his eyes, and holy shit there was a naked man standing in his living room. A naked man with strong calves and thick thighs. A decent-sized dick. Flat stomach. It didn't look like he ever worked out, but drag was supposed to be female illusion, so he had no reason to be a muscle-bound jock. But what froze Jack was the face. That gorgeous, naked face that he'd seen five days a week for the last three years. God, all of the similarities were there now that he'd seen the truth. How had he not seen it before?

"Ryan."

Ryan's bottom lip was trembling again. He looked like he wanted to run. Or vomit. But he stood his ground and held his head high. "Hey, Jack."

CHAPTER FOUR

Ryan felt more exposed than he ever had before. He usually didn't mind being naked—that was nothing. But with Jack standing only feet away, his face a mask of stunned disbelief, Ryan wanted to run and hide under a rock. He scratched the back of his neck, waiting for Jack to say something. Anything. The awkward silence stretched on until Ryan was practically choking on it. His skin crawled. He felt more like a freak now than he had the first time he'd put on a dress. What had made him think revealing himself would be a good idea? And after what had happened to Valentine? This was all too much.

"I knew this was a mistake," he said, turning so Jack hopefully wouldn't see how glassy his eyes were. He made a beeline for his clothes. He didn't care that he'd have to walk home looking like a man in a dress; he had to get out of here before things got any more humiliating.

"No. Ryan, wait."

Oh, *now* Jack had decided to find his voice. But it was too late. What if he told everyone? Ryan would never be able to show his face at the office again. And he didn't make nearly enough in tips to be a drag queen full-time. *I'll have to sell my body on the street and start calling myself Sparkle just to make rent. Maybe I'll be able to get a shitty apartment after I lose my house. God, how could I have been—*

Jack grabbed the bathroom door Ryan had been about to close. "Jesus, would you give me a second to process this before you go running off?"

Ryan chewed his bottom lip. "It was a dumb thing to do. And I knew that, but I did it anyway."

"It wasn't. I'm just surprised, is all. I mean seriously, how many dudes find out that they've been fucking their boss who's secretly a drag queen for the last two weeks?"

Ryan was going to be sick. He stepped away from the door and tried to head for the toilet, but Jack grabbed his hand and spun him around so they were facing each other. The lighting in here was crappy, and Jack was standing right beneath it; it illuminated him like an aura. He was fucking beautiful with that soft jawline, covered in a light dusting of scruff that always made Ryan want to cry because he could never grow it himself. Those deep, hazel eyes bore into his, and he still really wanted to leave, but the desire to stay was definitely gaining momentum.

"Yes," Jack said, "I'm kinda weirded out, but it's fine. I can deal."

"I'm not sure I can," Ryan whispered. Sure, Jack was looking at him with something akin to adoration right now, but what about tomorrow? Next week? Next month, if either one of them even made it that far? "No one at work knows. Hell, no one outside of the club knows. If this gets out, it would ruin me."

Jack shrugged. "Why would I tell anyone? I've got stuff that I don't want to get out, just like you do. So relax. It'll be our little secret."

Ryan wasn't sure he believed him, but he nodded anyway. The idea that he didn't have to keep his nightlife totally to himself now was comforting, even if what Jack said was a lie. But maybe it wasn't. Perhaps Jack would be able to keep his mouth shut and this could blossom into something great. Dysfunctional, but great.

"Fine," Ryan said.

"Good." Jack smiled. "Now let's go eat. It's getting cold."

"I'll be out in a second."

"Awesome." Jack backed out, not taking his eyes off Ryan, almost as though he was afraid he'd disappear.

When he was alone, Ryan looked at himself in the mirror. What had he gotten himself into? If he'd been able to control himself and had turned Jack away at the club that night, he wouldn't be in this position. But he also wouldn't be more sexually satisfied than he'd been since ever. Jack was the perfect lover—Ryan couldn't deny that, but something wasn't sitting right. Ryan didn't mind the secret thing at the moment, because hell, he wasn't exactly bursting at the seams to tell everyone his sexual proclivities, but how long would that last? He knew himself. Before long, he would start feeling weird about it. Because the truth was everyone would find out. Things done in the dark always came to light, and usually never in subtle ways. The question was: Would either of them be ready when the time rolled around?

The floor outside the bathroom creaked and snapped Ryan back to reality.

"You all right in there?" Jack called.

"Yeah, I'm fine. Just trying to get myself together."

"Okay."

Ryan scanned the room. No window to escape through if he decided that was his only option. The shower stall was only big enough for one, and the sink was lined with a toothbrush, shaving cream, razors, and a personal trimmer. The toothpaste sat on the other side. It was way tidier than his brother's bathroom and, for that, Ryan was thankful. He seemed to have a tight enough grip on himself now, so he took a deep breath and went to join Jack on the sofa.

But no sooner had he sat down than unease started creeping up his spine, tensing his shoulders, and warming his skin. He was still ass-naked, open to far more scrutiny than if he'd been in full geish.

"I . . . um . . ." He swallowed, throat suddenly bone-dry. It shouldn't be this hard to find words. He looked down at the ground. "I wasn't really expecting to stay the night, so . . . I didn't bring anything to change into . . ."

Jack was wider in the waist than he was. And the shoulders. Anything he tried to put on would drown him in a millisecond.

He could feel the color rising in his cheeks. Surely, this embarrassment would subside sooner or later. But if it didn't and he still felt like a self-conscious boob after Jack fell asleep, he'd sneak out. Maybe borrow a hoodie or something and speak in his best Sheila voice so whatever cabbie or Uber driver that took him home didn't get suspicious.

"I've got a couple tees that'd probably fit you and a pair of shorts, or two." There was laughter in Jack's voice. Ryan didn't think he was being laughed at, but couldn't be sure, so he kept his head down. "I'll go grab them. You want to come with or want me to just bring them out?"

"I can stay here. Thanks."

Jack got up and disappeared.

Ryan covered his crotch with his hands. This was one of the reasons he liked being Sheila so much. She wasn't fearless, not by a long shot, but she was a damn shot more outgoing and confident than he was. She was a better version of him. It didn't matter that he made her up; the only thing that mattered was that she did the trick. He sometimes pretended to be her in court, and those were usually the cases where his courtroom etiquette was most noticed, for better or worse. He kept hoping that someday her personality would bleed into his. But it hadn't happened, yet.

Jack came back a few seconds later. "These should fit you, I think. I outgrew them ages ago."

"So why do you still have them?" Ryan asked, taking them. "And thank you."

"Laundry day."

Ryan chuckled as he slid into the shorts. Thank God for elastic waistbands. The silky fabric whispered over his skin like an old lover. They were foreign, but comfortable. The shirt was a better fit. It hugged his upper arms, but otherwise it was perfect. He gave Jack a grateful nod.

"I should warm this up," Jack said, picking up the plates and shuffling off toward the kitchen.

"You're sure this is okay?" Ryan asked, massaging the inside of his wrist.

"Relax. I want you to stay, all right? It's fine."

Ryan nodded. He settled back on the couch and drew his legs up to his chest. Valentine used to tell him that things would be fine all the time. Whenever he was having one of his breakdowns and crises of confidence, she would always calm him. Make him a cup of tea, tell him that everything would be okay and then, if those methods failed, she told him to buck up, put on his big-girl clothes, and get the shit done. God, he couldn't believe she was gone.

The tears came again, slowly at first, but by the time Jack came back, Ryan was sobbing uncontrollably. This wasn't fair. Who would want to hurt her? Valentine—Tim—was one of the most gentle people he knew. Always there to lend a helping hand or dig someone out of a hole they found themselves in or a problem they'd managed to work their way into. She was an amazing human being. For someone to butcher her and then leave her body in a dumpster . . . it was the ultimate disrespect.

Jack put a hand on his back. Ryan wanted to shake it off, but couldn't find the strength. So he let himself be pulled into Jack's embrace.

The worst of the breakdown passed quickly, and then he was weeping quietly into Jack's shoulder. He took a few deep breaths. When he thought he had himself under control, he sat up again.

"I'm sorry I keep crying like this. I just . . ."

"You don't have to explain anything. I understand." Jack wiped away more of Ryan's tears.

The same way Valentine used to. Another wave of sorrow wracked him, but he held his composure. He kept it together. He wouldn't lose it again. But a moment later he did. Again and again until there couldn't be any emotion left in his body. He lay back, too weak to move or even open his eyes, while Jack went to get him a glass of water. Their dinner sat all but forgotten on the table, but Ryan didn't have an appetite. He didn't think he'd ever want to eat again.

"Open up," Jack said. Ryan did as he was told and, a moment later, a cool rush of water filled his mouth. He gulped it down. He couldn't remember water ever tasting so good. It didn't bring back any of his sapped energy, but it cleared the fog from his head. His breathing became normal again. He took a deep breath, opened his eyes the tiniest sliver.

"Thank you," he said hoarsely. "I'm . . . I'm really glad I'm not alone right now." He nestled against Jack; the warmth was comforting.

He wasn't sure how long they sat there, or how many times he drifted off, but he felt it when Jack got up. He heard him stretch and then walk away. Ryan couldn't bring himself to open his eyes, though. It would be so much easier to just stay like this forever. Curled up on this sofa, knowing nothing of the world beyond these four walls. But that couldn't happen. He had a life he'd have to get back to whether he liked it or not. A life of secrets. A life of hidden identities. A life where he no longer had a best friend. But he'd get through it and stand tall, because he didn't have a choice. It was what everyone expected of him and what he expected of himself.

A minute later he heard Jack coming. Jack settled back in and draped a blanket over both of them. The sound of a *Golden Girls* rerun filled the room, and Ryan cuddled a little closer. He wanted to think he could get used to this: sitting with someone he cared about, no expectations, no nothing. But how real was that? How long could it last?

No. It was better to keep himself as emotionally detached from the man next to him as possible. That way neither of them would wind up hurt. But as snores made Jack's chest rumble and Ryan found a smile pulling at the corners of his mouth, he realized it was already too late.

Ryan woke up to the smell of pancakes, bacon, and eggs. He sniffed hopefully at the air as he sat up and stretched before lying back down. He shut his eyes and tried to savor this moment.

"Morning, sleepy," Jack said.

Ryan opened his eyes again. Jack was standing in the kitchen, shirtless. He flashed Ryan a smile before turning around.

"What time is it?" Ryan asked.

"Little after ten. Figured you could use the sleep, so I got up and made breakfast."

"Thanks," Ryan said as Jack handed him a glass of orange juice before heading back into the kitchen. His ass filled out those Grinch pajama bottoms nicely.

Ryan wasn't used to sleeping this late. It was disorienting, to say the least. Even though it was Saturday, he usually would have had his nose buried in a case by now, or be making an outfit for one of Sheila's shows.

He took a sip of his drink; it was more bitter than he would have liked, but he was grateful, nonetheless. "So are you one of those guys who ran out to get all this while I was out of it?"

"Nope. I get up every morning and make breakfast for myself, for your information. So I'm just adding a little extra to the pan."

Ryan nodded appreciatively. "Impressive."

"Well, it was either cook for myself or spend all my cash on takeout, and that wasn't about to happen."

Jack came back with two plates and sat them down on the table, then headed toward the kitchen again. It had been a while since Ryan had had a spread like this. Not only was there what he'd already smelled, but there was sausage, hash browns, and fruit. Ryan eyed Jack suspiciously as he returned with silverware and napkins. "You eat like this every day?" That couldn't be true. Jack's physique would have shown it, and there didn't seem to be a gram of fat anywhere other than his dick and ass.

"Of course not. But I'm not a savage. I didn't know what you'd like, so I made it all."

Jack's eyes flitted away, then back to Ryan's just as quickly. Ryan tilted his head and inspected the man in front of him. "Are you okay?"

Jack cleared his throat. "Yeah, I'm great."

Ryan wasn't convinced, but he tucked the thought away as Jack sat down next to him. They ate in relative silence, watching cartoons and occasionally stealing glances at one another. Something felt off, but Ryan couldn't put his finger on what it was. Unsure whether to move closer, or scoot away, he settled for shoveling a forkful of eggs into his mouth and halfheartedly watching Jackie Chan battle an army of demon sorcerers.

When they were done, Jack carted the dishes away.

"Thank you. For last night, I mean," Ryan said, scratching the back of his neck. "I don't know what I would have done if I'd been alone when I found out."

"No problem. How're you feeling?"

Ryan shrugged. It felt like his heart had been ripped from his chest. Valentine had been an amazing friend and such an important part of his life. She'd been such a good person. No matter how hard he tried, he couldn't think of a single reason for someone to want to hurt her. "I still don't want to believe it. But I'm dealing."

"That's good."

"I can't even look at my phone, though. It was buzzing all night, and I'm sure it's people wanting to check on me and tell me what happened and I . . . It's too much right now."

"You don't think they'll be worried?"

"I'll call them back. I just need some time."

Neither of them spoke while Jack washed the dishes. Ryan was starting to feel awkward. He shouldn't have stayed here. It would have been smarter to go home, because then at least he could figure things out in his own bed and not have to try to force conversation. He was about to tell Jack he was going to head out when Jack came out of the kitchen, drying his hands on a rag.

"I'm gonna head to the gym in a little bit. You're welcome to come with me, if you want."

"Nah, I'm okay. I was actually about to head home."

"Oh." Was that disappointment in Jack's eyes? "Well did you want to catch a movie later, or something?"

"I don't know."

Jack ran a hand through his hair. "I actually really like spending time with you. Kinda want to get to know you better."

"Really?" Ryan didn't think he'd ever heard that before. He'd had (sort of) boyfriends before, yeah, but none of them had seemed to care enough to try to get to know the real him.

"Yeah. I mean, if you want. If you think it'll be weird, I can back off." But Jack didn't look too sure of that.

"No, it's fine. A movie sounds great."

There was the smile that Ryan was getting so used to. It could light up an entire city. "Awesome. I'm gonna get ready and then we can head out together."

"Sounds like a plan," Ryan said. Then it dawned on him he didn't have anything to wear home. And no makeup here, so there was no way he was wearing the outfit he'd showed up in. "Um, do you think I could maybe borrow a pair of sweats until I get home?"

"Sure. I'll grab them while I'm back there." Jack headed toward his bedroom.

Ryan got up and followed. He couldn't take sitting there any longer. He stopped just short of Jack's door, though. Jack had already kicked off his pajama bottoms, and his ass was staring at Ryan, practically begging to be fondled. Jack threw a towel over his shoulder and turned around, but paused when he saw Ryan. "Sorry," he said. "Didn't hear you sneak up."

"No need to apologize," Ryan said. "I was only gonna ask if I could come in, but then you were standing there naked and I just forgot everything." Jack laughed. Ryan ran a hand through his hair; it was a nervous habit he'd always had trouble shaking. "Hey, what do you say we have a little quickie before we go our separate ways?"

Jack opened his mouth and his gaze flitted away again. "I actually wanted to get there before it gets too crowded. Rain check?"

"Um, yeah. Sure."

"Thanks. You can chill in here until I get out, no problem. Sweats are in the bottom drawer." And he squeezed past Ryan and into the hallway.

Ryan hated being shot down. It always made him feel like such a creep for asking in the first place. He plopped on Jack's bed as the shower started. Maybe he should sneak out, avoid the awkwardness that would no doubt hang in the air as they rode the elevator. But even though his pride said to cut his losses and make a run for it, his heart wouldn't let him. Not like he was falling in love this quickly or anything crazy like that, but there was definitely a spark. Jack hadn't gone running when he found out that Sheila was Ryan, and that made all the difference in the world. Jack didn't make him feel like a circus act. He didn't stare or point, so Ryan owed him better than sneaking off.

So Ryan waited.

Jack came back fifteen minutes later, body glistening.

Ryan stared, throat suddenly dry. He couldn't remember how to breathe. Or swallow. Jack's muscles seemed extra large and magnetic because, no matter how hard he tried, Ryan couldn't tear his eyes away from them. Jack sauntered forward, until his dick was eye level with Ryan.

"We've got five minutes. Turn over."

He was on his hands and knees before Jack finished his sentence. Jack probed Ryan's hole with a slick finger, but he didn't do much prepping. Ryan didn't mind; he liked the stretch and burn as Jack slid inside him.

"Don't make a sound," Jack ordered. He grabbed hold of Ryan's hips and went to work, but not even a minute later he started going soft. He slowed and then stopped, cursing.

"What is it?" Ryan asked, glancing back. Jack's shoulders slumped. He stared up at the ceiling, mouth twisting in a grimace. But his face had turned a deep red. When he looked back down, there was something in his eyes Ryan couldn't quite read. "What's wrong?"

"I thought . . . I mean . . . I just figured . . ." He turned around. He ran a frustrated hand through his hair as he headed toward the dresser.

"Are you okay?" Ryan asked. "Did I do something?"

"No. You're fine," Jack said, tossing a pair of sweat pants and a T-shirt in Ryan's direction. His shoulders were tensed, and his neck had turned a bright red. Veins stuck out in the backs of his arms, and Ryan wondered if he was gripping the edges of the dresser. "It's all me. I promise."

That didn't inspire confidence, but Ryan didn't push the subject, simply got dressed and made a beeline for the living room. He knew he should have left. If he had, that would have never happened, and he wouldn't feel like he wanted to crawl into a hole and die right now. He kinda believed Jack when he said it had been a personal problem, but that didn't mean Ryan would ever be able to look him in the eye again. *Maybe I should just email the other partners my resignation right now.*

No, he told the voice in his head. *Relax and don't go there. Everything is fine.*

So why didn't anything feel fine? He massaged his chest, where a dim emotional despair had begun to settle. And of course, he'd left his anxiety meds at home. Fuck.

"Hey," Jack said. Ryan turned around as Jack pulled a tank top over his head. "It's nothing to worry about. Really." He slung his gym bag on his shoulder. "You ready?"

Ryan nodded. He didn't trust himself to speak yet.

Jack gave him a half smile, and they left the apartment.

Halfway down to the lobby, a fresh wave of sorrow rolled over Ryan as he realized, once again, that Valentine was dead. She was the one he'd usually call when he needed to talk his way through an attack, no matter how mild. But he wouldn't let himself cry in front of Jack again. Not right now, anyway. That would only make things worse. So he held his tears back, bid Jack farewell as soon as the elevator doors opened, and darted for the exit. Outside in the cool morning air, he let his tears fall.

He didn't stop crying for the rest of the day.

CHAPTER FIVE

Jack shuffled through the papers on his desk for the hundredth time, expecting something different. But it was a known fact that if something wasn't there the first time, it usually wouldn't appear out of nowhere because you decided to search again. This was a law firm. Not Hogwarts. He couldn't even remember what he was hunting for. A deposition? Discovery file? He heaved a sigh and scrubbed a hand over his face. Why was his brain so all over the place lately?

Because you're a piece of shit, a little voice in his mind supplied. He rolled his eyes and looked up in time to see Ryan walk past his office without even glancing inside. For the fifth time today. He deserved that, he supposed. The two of them had met up a couple of times in the week since Ryan left him standing in the elevator, but it hadn't been the same. They hadn't had sex at all and the conversation had been strained. No matter what Jack said, Ryan wouldn't believe that he wasn't the problem. And Jack couldn't tell him the truth about why he'd stopped fucking him senseless.

How did you tell someone you couldn't sleep with them when they weren't in drag because you can't keep your dick hard? Even thinking it made Jack's skin crawl, so how would Ryan feel actually *hearing* it? No. Jack wouldn't do that to him. He'd have to figure out a way around it. Especially because he was starting to miss the company. But what to say?

He pulled his phone out of his desk and debated texting Ryan. That was so impersonal, though. Ryan was right up the hall, so why not grow a pair, walk up, and talk to him like a fucking person instead of hiding behind the safety of a screen?

Jack got up, but froze before he could leave his safe zone. Because once he left this room, he wouldn't let himself turn back until they talked. And that wouldn't be a bad thing, but for whatever reason his palms were slick with sweat and his stomach knotted, and fuck, he did not have to piss this bad a few seconds ago. He tried to shake the nerves away and imagine what he'd do if he were Sheila. Or any woman, for that matter. Women were braver. They faced their problems head on instead of dicking around in their office like a scared puppy. He needed to woman up and get it over with.

He made it to the door before he chickened out. Why didn't he just cut his balls off and put them in a jar somewhere, because they weren't doing him any good right now. Jack went back to his desk, but before he could sit down, the phone rang.

"Yes, Michelle?"

"Mr. Swift would like to see you in his office," his assistant told him.

Jack's heart dropped into his feet. They were going to have that conversation no matter how terrified he was. "Okay. Thank you," he croaked, and hung up. "Well played, universe."

He straightened his jacket and walked out into the hallway.

Ryan's office was only around the corner, but the floor seemed to stretch on for miles, and with every step Jack's tie got a little tighter. He'd been going for two, seven, nine hours; he'd need to stop and pitch a tent for the night soon. But finally Ryan's door came into view, only an ocean of associates away. He could make it. Maybe.

He knocked lightly on the open door. Ryan looked up. There was no spark. No lust. Barely even recognition. Jack had royally fucked this up, and he wasn't sure how to fix it. He cleared his throat. "Michelle said you wanted to see me, sir?"

Something seemed to flash through Ryan's eyes, but it passed too quickly for Jack to read. Had he imagined it?

"Yes," Ryan said. "Please come in."

Jack did as he was told, resisting the urge to close the door behind him. He took a seat across from his boss (drag queen. Friend. Lover?) and folded his hands in his lap.

Ryan inspected him for a moment. "I wanted to talk to you about the Benning case."

Jack nodded. "Okay."

Ryan started talking, but Jack didn't hear anything he said. He kept replaying that morning in his apartment and the defeated, confused look on Ryan's face as he jetted from the room. Jack had wanted to tell him then, but hadn't been able to find the words. Even now, he still couldn't, and the more time he let pass, the worse things were going to be for him. He knew that from experience. Jack wanted to keep hanging out with Ryan. God knew he did. And he wanted to keep nailing him, because who wouldn't want to fuck an ass that perfect on a person who had next to no inhibitions? He'd have to be crazy to want to let that go. But it wasn't fair to make Ryan dress up just so they could have sex if he didn't want to. It wasn't right. And Jack wouldn't hurt Ryan like that.

He didn't know what he was going to do. Or how to go about this. But he did know that he desperately wanted some alone time with his boss away from this fucking building. Alone time that wasn't peppered with awkward silences and covert glances that stopped as soon as the other person looked your way. Even if they just went to a fucking bar and got drinks.

Ryan snapped his fingers in front of Jack's face. "Earth to Jack! Are you even listening to me?"

"What?" Jack blinked several times and shook himself back to reality.

Ryan drew his lips into the tightest line Jack had ever seen. "What's so important that you can't pay attention for five fucking minutes?"

Jack held Ryan's gaze for the first time since he'd walked in. He licked his lips, took a deep breath, and said, "You."

"Excuse me?" Ryan raised an eyebrow.

Jack lowered his voice. "Look, I'm sorry about last week and how weird it's been since then, but if you let me explain—"

"This is not the place for this," Ryan said through gritted teeth. His whole demeanor had changed, and suddenly Jack was afraid of the man in front of him. After all, on a professional level, Ryan held Jack's entire life in his hands. "Besides, you've had more than enough time to explain. If you can't even be honest with me, I'm not interested in anything you have to say."

"You're right." Jack hated how timid his voice sounded. "About everything. So meet me after work tonight at Icefire. I promise you I'll explain as much as I can."

Icefire was a bar not far from his place. It was far enough out of the way that he didn't think they'd be recognized, but popular enough that they could be lost in the crowd.

"Sheila has a show tonight."

"Then meet me before. Or after. Please. I miss spending time with you, man."

There it was again. That same flash from before. But Jack knew what it was this time. Doubt.

"Please," Jack repeated. "Don't make me start quoting Britney. Cuz I'll do it."

"Fine," Ryan said, cracking a smile for the first time since Jack had walked in. It filled Jack with a subtle warmth.

"Thank you."

"Don't thank me. You're not out of the doghouse yet."

Jack grinned. "But I will be."

"We'll see about that."

Jack relaxed; it felt like days since the last time he had. "You wanna run that info about the case by me again?"

Ryan's eyes narrowed. "I've got a meeting to get to, so I'll shoot you an email."

"Okay. That's fine."

"I know it is," Ryan said with his head cocked to the side. "Now get the hell out of my office."

Jack's face stretched in a smile. "Yes, sir." He stood up.

"And stop calling me sir."

Jack wanted to lean forward and whisper his response, but people were probably passing behind him every few seconds, so instead he lowered his voice and said, "Would you rather I called you ma'am?"

"Fuck you," Ryan growled playfully.

Jack went on his way, and the walk back to his own office was much shorter. He fell into the plushy chair in the corner of his office and breathed a sigh of relief. The hardest part had been setting up the talk. Now that that was done, though, he still had to figure out what in the name of Chuck Shurley he was going to say. But he had time to work on that. Or to chicken out and risk Ryan never speaking to him again. He wasn't going to let that happen, though. He pulled his cell from his pocket and sent Ryan a message.

See you tonight.

Jack stood outside Icefire, his insides doing the hokey-pokey. Maybe Ryan wasn't coming. He'd probably only said he was to get Jack off his back. Jack pulled his shirt down again. The tighter it was stretched, the better his chest would look and the less likely Ryan would be able to resist him. But that only worked if Ryan showed up. He checked his watch. Quarter past eight. Sheila's show started at ten, so they didn't have a lot of time. Getting in drag couldn't be a quick thing; all the makeup and hair and tucking. How long would Ryan need to become Sheila?

Jack was about to just go inside and grab a drink, when he spotted his boss walking around the corner. He smiled without meaning to, his entire face growing warm.

"Hey," Ryan said as he approached. "Sorry I'm late. I had to stay back at the office and lost track of time."

"It's fine. I'm just glad you came." Jack held the door open and they went in. They found a table on the other side of the bar and settled in. There was a basketball game on the TV, but Jack couldn't hear what they were saying. The air reeked more of booze than usual, and there was a steady hum of conversation that he was grateful for.

"Do you want a beer or . . .?" he asked Ryan.

"Whiskey soda," Ryan said. "I like to have a light buzz going when I'm putting on my makeup."

The corner of Jack's mouth quirked up in a grin. "You got it."

He went up to the bartender and put in their order. His skin buzzed as he leaned on the counter and waited. He'd spent an hour getting ready and then another fifteen minutes standing outside the bar before he'd even gotten here. Now that he had what he wanted—at least for the night—he didn't know what to say. Or how to bring it up. He looked over his shoulder and saw Ryan inspecting his fingernails—maybe he was sizing them up for press-ons. He hadn't made a run for it, though. That was a start. If Ryan was brave enough to be here, then Jack could be too. But when he got the drinks and headed back to the table, time did that weird warp thing again, and it felt like seven days and seven nights before he sat down and pushed Ryan's whiskey soda toward him.

He sipped his own vodka cranberry, racking his brains for something, anything to talk about to break the ice.

"So why are we here?" Ryan asked after gulping down his drink.

Right. Straight to the point, then. Jack took another moment (or maybe it was closer to ten. He couldn't be totally sure at this point) to compose himself. "About the other morning . . ." Ryan nodded, watching him with a cynical expression, like he'd heard it all before and was only sticking around to see how creative Jack's excuse was. "I meant it when I said it wasn't you. Not completely, anyway." Ryan tilted his head and his gaze turned inquisitive. "The truth is I couldn't keep my dick hard, okay? It felt great at first, but then I looked down and I just couldn't keep it up."

"What are you saying? What happened when you looked down?"

"I saw . . . you . . ."

Ryan nodded, dragged his bottom lip between his teeth. His eyes darted toward the exit, then back to Jack, then down at the table. Jack could swear those were tears growing fat at the corners, and that was a knife slicing white-hot through his own gut.

"It was a mental thing!" he said quickly. "My brain is stupid and it's all my fucking parents' fault. Literally the only problem was that you looked like a dude."

Ryan sniffled. "What the fuck is that supposed to mean?"

"Look . . . growing up . . . my entire life all my family ever told me was how wrong it is to be gay. And they think being bi is even worse. My aunt and my uncle on my dad's side disowned my cousin and practically beat him to death just because he said he wasn't leaving home. My sister got arrested for breaking the hand of a girl who she thought was flirting with her, even though she wasn't. I talked to the girl. She was just trying to be nice because she thought my sister needed a friend." Jack chewed the inside of his cheek. "My parents preached fire and brimstone and went on and on about how unnatural it is, and so when I found myself seeing guys that way, I freaked."

Jack took a deep breath, let it out as slow as he could. He ran a hand over his head and took another swig. "I didn't know what to do. I didn't want to lose my family, so I hid it. I had girlfriends and brought them home to meet everyone and we fooled around and it was nice. I even really liked a few of them. I just . . . I kept wondering what it would be like to be with a guy. But I was terrified, so I never tried anything. And the girls . . . they . . . I dunno sensed, maybe, that something was wrong. I wasn't giving them my all, or even my three-quarters, and they all left me. I've spent most of my life alone."

Jack stared down into his cup. There were only a few cubes of ice left, and even those had started to melt. His drink wasn't red anymore, so much as a deep pink. He blinked away tears, because he'd never told anyone this before and he hadn't been ready for how much ripping the bandage off his past had *stung*. The walls were crumbling down, and he didn't know how to stop them, so he kept talking. "Even through college, I just couldn't do it. Every time I thought about it . . . every time I tried . . . I'd get close and I couldn't get over the fact that they were dudes and it was a total boner killer. At least, I thought it was because they were dudes. Back then I didn't even truly understand why. All I knew was I had these feelings and I wanted to have sex with these guys, and I couldn't. I'd be at full-mast and ready to go when I thought about it and even when I was about to do it. And then I'd get in the moment and . . . feathers were harder than I was. I always thought guys were supposed to be able to get it up and fuck whenever."

He looked up at Ryan to find his boss's (friend's?) mouth hanging the slightest bit open and his eyes sparkling with tears. "You're the first man I ever slept with. And as shitty as it is to say, the only reason I was able to do it is because you were Sheila. I sought you out because you were Sheila and I *needed* to know what it felt like to fuck a guy at least once before I turn thirty, and if you'd shot me down that night, I don't know what I would have done."

Ryan scoffed playfully. "I didn't know I had that much power."

"Yeah, well, you did. I can keep a hard-on when I'm with Sheila because she looks like a woman. I can trick my brain, I guess. I'm trying to get past it, but I need you to give me a little more time. I mean, we don't have to have sex whenever we see each other. We can hang out. I'm not trying to pressure you, or anything. I wouldn't even ask, because I know it's a shit thing to do. But somewhere along the line I started to really like hanging out with you, and now it makes me feel like shit that I might have ruined that."

"You didn't ruin anything," Ryan said, shaking his head. "I wish you'd said something that morning, is all. Since then I've been feeling like a fool and I didn't know what was going on or what to do."

"I'm sorry. I got pissed off and then I panicked and I . . ." Jack sighed. "I didn't know how to say any of this."

"And here I thought my family was a train wreck."

Jack chuckled. He felt lighter than he had in days, and now all he wanted to do was spend the rest of the night reconnecting and making up for lost time. "Yeah, mine is fucking crazy."

"Oh no, so is mine." Ryan looked at his watch. "But we're gonna have to save that story for another time. I gotta get to the club and start getting ready."

It was barely quarter till. "How long does it take you?" Jack asked, standing.

"Honestly? I like to have at least two hours."

Jack stared at him, agog. *Two hours?* He didn't think there was that much makeup in the world.

Ryan chuckled. "But in a pinch, I can do my makeup in about forty-five minutes. That's only in extreme cases, though. Cuz then I don't get to put a lot of effort into much else."

Jack nodded. It still didn't make any sense to him, but he'd keep his mouth shut.

Ryan smiled at him again. "Walk me there?"

"Absolutely." As they left the bar, Jack breathed a sigh of relief. It was nice to have an easygoing conversation after a week of nothing but strain. He wanted to reach out and take Ryan's hand. But he resisted the urge. Just in case anyone from the office happened to be out and about. That was one scandal they didn't need right now.

Besides, he was perfectly fine with how things were for the moment. Walking and talking and laughing and joking. He felt right in a way he hadn't in a long time, and he didn't want to give it up for anything. So whatever he had to do to push past his barrier, he'd do it, if that was what Ryan needed him to do. For now, as they walked in the rear door of Neon Trees, Jack would hang in the crowd and enjoy the show. And, God willing, the aftershow, because he was beyond backed-up.

He just hoped Ryan wouldn't mind staying dressed a little while longer.

INTERLUDE UNKNOWN

The blood from his severed jugular spurted in my face; every pump of his slowing heart sent another jet, though they got less and less. After a moment, he crumpled to the ground, lifeless eyes staring at the sky, the ghost of his final words on his lips. I growled, low in my throat and gripped my cock through my jeans. God, I wanted to stroke one out right here, right now, but it was too risky. Instead, I pulled a rag from my back pocket and wiped the gore first from my face and then from my knife. I scrubbed the inside of my shirt over my skin to try to get rid of any left behind.

I slipped my phone from my pocket and checked my face in the camera. It was still a little red, but the night was dark. No moon out casting that eerie glow. I could keep to the shadows. And I needed to get a nut. But I also wanted to kill again.

Tucking the knife away, I slipped out of the alleyway and joined the flow of people. They had no clue what had just happened only a few feet from them; that made me hornier, for some reason. I didn't know where I was going, but my feet seemed to be carrying me somewhere, so I followed their lead, sizing up the people around me as I went.

The guy next to me could probably kick my ass. The scowl on his face said he wasn't to be fucked with. The woman ahead of me looked like she carried weapons in her purse. A dozen people I checked as I walked, but none of them made my pulse jump the way the bitch walking out of the club earlier tonight had. I'd known it had been a man; it had been painfully obvious even under the ten pounds of makeup. I'd found my next victim. My mouth had practically been watering as I'd followed him, chatted him up, and when he'd realized that he was going to die . . . God, the look on his face had been better than Christmas.

Maybe I had a type.

I blinked myself back to reality and, for a moment, didn't know where I was. I looked around for a few seconds before my eyes adjusted and saw the headstones in the darkness. Of course. I was back at the cemetery where the first one was buried.

I'd been here during the funeral too. And no one had even noticed me.

Oh well. Since I'd come all this way, I might as well make the most of it.

CHAPTER SIX

Ryan emptied the bag of imitation rhinestones into his bowl. He ran a thumb over the ceramic surface and smiled. The bowl was one of the first things his drag mother Justine had ever given him. *"Nobody likes a messy queen,"* she'd said. *"So make sure you always keep your materials together. Especially when you get on that RuPaul show."*

He put his shoe, a simple, sleek boot with a five-inch heel, on the table in front of him and leaned in with the glue. A lot of queens would probably have someone else do this for them, but he actually liked making all his own stuff. The art of taking and combining things to create something entirely new calmed him. Maybe it was the time it took, or being forced to focus so he didn't fuck it up. It didn't matter. Costuming was one of the best parts of doing drag for him, and he didn't understand queens who hated it.

He secured the first stone to the shoe and already he'd started to slip into his zone. Part of his mind zeroed in on the task at hand, but the bit that was already creating and dreaming began to wander.

After he and Jack had their talk and Sheila finished her show, the two of them had headed to Jack's apartment, and Ryan had felt almost peaceful. Being around Jack for the past couple weeks had been easy, most of the time. Ryan hadn't had to try too hard, or kiss anyone's ass, or try to be anyone he wasn't. The only real problem was having to dress up to fuck. Ryan had to spend twice as long on his wigs, now, because they kept getting messed up during sex and then he had to restyle them.

He'd never had such a relaxing relationship (Though it *definitely* wasn't a romantic one. Not yet, anyway.) before and it felt strange. Almost as though the sky was bound to come crashing down on their heads, and they were treading water, waiting.

But other than that, they were golden.

His phone rang, and he fished it out of his pocket, expecting it to be Jack. But no, Justine's face smiled up at him, and he couldn't help but grin as he answered it. "Bitch, I've been trying to call you for four days! Where the hell have you been?"

Justine cleared her throat, and the sound was deeper than Ryan was used to. "Hey, kid."

He rarely heard that voice, anymore. It was a man's voice, heavy with emotion. Which meant that he was talking to Danny. The drag persona had been caged, and that could only mean bad news.

"What's wrong?"

"It's about Valentine."

Ryan blinked. How could it get worse than being murdered and thrown in a dumpster? "What about her?"

Danny heaved a sigh. "Someone vandalized her headstone last night."

Ryan shook his head. He hadn't heard that right. "I'm sorry, what?"

"You heard me. Somebody went to the cemetery last night. They found Tim's grave and they went to town on it."

"How?"

"Spray-painted over it. Wrote 'Faggots burn in hell.' And then took a shit right in front of it."

That piqued Ryan's interest. Maybe that could be used for DNA and the police would catch whoever did this. He wiped away a tear. "How'd you find out?"

"Because I came to put down some more flowers and saw it."

"You're there now?"

"Yes."

"I'm on my way," he said, getting up.

"No. I don't want you seeing this, kid. The police are heading here, already. I just wanted you to hear it from me and not on the news."

"Who would do something like this?" Ryan sniffled. Hadn't Tim suffered enough?

"The same kind of monster who killed her. But don't worry. The cops are going to find out who did it."

"How? They're probably miles away by now!"

Danny was silent for a moment. "I have faith. I have to. Otherwise I have to accept that none of us are safe. And I'm not ready to do that, yet."

That was a scary thought. What if it had been the same person? And what if they decided to kill again? But no. Ryan shook the thought away. Serial killers were one in a hundred. And there were better places to start a spree than here. "I understand. Thanks for calling."

"Yeah," Danny said, and disconnected.

Ryan hated this world. Why couldn't people just leave them be? They weren't doing anything to anyone. He stared down at the rhinestone-covered boot on his desk. The thought of finishing it sickened him. For the first time in six years, he wanted nothing to do with performing in drag. But Valentine would have kicked his ass if he gave up because of someone else. Even if that someone had slaughtered her. So he dredged his way through and finished it, stopping every so often to wipe away tears.

The boots turned out more killer than he could have imagined, but his mind still wasn't clear. If anything, it raced even faster. His heart thundered and his blood pounded in his veins. He needed a distraction. Something to make him think about literally anything else.

Jack picked up on the third ring. "Hey."

"I need you. Like right now."

"What's the matter?"

"My mouth is empty. And you're still at home asking me questions."

"I'm on my way."

Ryan managed a small smile. At least sex worked for him. But now that he'd made the call and Jack was on his way, Ryan didn't want to get dressed up. And that would almost certainly be a deal breaker. Even after all this time.

It had only been a couple weeks since their conversation at Icefire, but they'd hooked up countless times over the last month and a half, and still the drag had to come out. Ryan hated that, but it was either get dressed up and get some dick, or stay as he was and keep thinking about Valentine and having mini-breakdowns every fifteen minutes.

So he got up and headed off to the drag closet, shoes in one hand and materials in the other.

By the time Jack got there twenty minutes later, Ryan was in the quickest drag he'd ever done. But he didn't feel the elation that usually came with getting done up. Instead, it was something like dread, and as he dropped to his knees and went to work, it felt more like a chore than anything.

The sex was good; Jack didn't know how to do it any other way. But Ryan's brain wouldn't let him enjoy it as much as he wanted to. When they were done and cleaned up, Ryan sat on the edge of his bed with his chin in his hand, chewing his bottom lip.

"What's the matter?" Jack asked, pulling his shirt on. Ryan looked up and lost his breath for a second. The way the sunlight hit Jack cast him in an almost angelic glow, and fuck if he wasn't more gorgeous than usual. Ryan blinked, trying to break the trance he was slipping into. Maybe if he turned away, he'd be able to speak.

"How do you really feel about me?" Ryan asked, eyes trained on a photo on his dresser behind Jack.

"What do you mean?"

"I mean . . . what is this? What are we? Is this a friends-with-benefits type situation? Are we friends at all? Is it just fucking? Are you my boyfriend? What's going on?"

"Whoa, where is all this coming from?"

Ryan suddenly felt stupid. This wasn't the right time to bring this up, but he'd already opened the can of worms, now. He couldn't close it again. "It's coming from me wanting to know. It's getting really fucking irritating having to get dressed up every time I want to get some dick."

"Hold on, you called me. I didn't ask to come over here."

"But you came! I called because I was upset. And then I realized I was gonna have to put on a dress and a wig and I didn't want to do it anymore, but you were already on the way."

"So why didn't you say something when I got here?"

"Because I didn't want to be that . . . asshole," Ryan said lamely. He curled his tongue in his mouth. Tears built behind his eyes, but he wouldn't give in to them.

Jack knelt in front of him. "You wouldn't have been an asshole. The same way you're ambushing me with this now, you could have told me when I walked through the door and we . . . could have talked or something."

Their eyes met and Ryan forced himself not to look away. "I really like you. But this morning got super hard for a minute. And that's when I called you. I called you over here so you could fuck me and make me forget for a little while. I just didn't think before about what it was going to entail."

Jack dropped his gaze. "I'm working on it. I promise you I am. I just . . . I need time."

"But how much? I don't know how long I can keep feeling like I have to do this if I want to have sex with you."

"I don't know . . ." Jack stood up, scratching his head. "Maybe we should cool off a bit. I don't want to make you feel uncomfortable. Because you don't have to do anything you don't want to, and I don't want you to think you do. I'm not that kind of guy. And the truth is, I like you too."

"Then go on a date with me." Ryan's mouth said it before his brain could process the thought, and he regretted it almost immediately.

Jack blinked, his lips parted. "A . . ." He cleared his throat. "A what?"

Ryan swallowed. It took him a second to draw the breath to speak again but he had to. "I want you to go on a date with me. Doesn't have to be fancy, but I want to do it."

"I don't know if I'm ready for that . . ." Jack said, running a hand through his hair. "Is it a deal breaker if I don't?"

Ryan's heart sank. So this *was* just sex. Once again he'd let himself fall for someone who didn't feel the same, and fuck if he didn't seem like the dumbest person on the planet. Again. When would he learn? "No," he said, avoiding Jack's eyes. "No, of course not." But he didn't know if he meant that. He tried to swallow the lump in his throat and failed.

He wanted to cry. And scream. And vomit. But he couldn't do any of that in front of Jack, so he turned away and tried to hide from the wave of emotion that threatened to overwhelm him. He needed to get some privacy so he could break down in peace, but if he kicked

Jack out now, Jack would know the truth, and Ryan didn't want to look weak. So he fought back the tears and forced himself to grow a pair, even if they were only pretend.

"I'll do it," Jack said.

Ryan spun around, eyes wide. "What?"

Jack closed his eyes. "I think a date is a bad idea. And I'm not totally sure that I'm ready for it, but I really like you. And I don't want to lose you, and I feel like that's what we're heading toward."

"Jack . . ."

"I'll go on a date with you."

"Really?" Ryan didn't want Jack to feel obligated, but he was having a hard time trying to contain his excitement.

"If it'll make you happy, yeah. Of course."

"But . . . it'll make you happy too . . . right?"

The corner of Jack's mouth quirked up in a sad imitation of a smile. "I don't know, yet. But the only way to find out is to try."

"Only if you want to."

Jack nodded slowly. "I want to."

He didn't look sure, but Ryan wasn't going to press the issue any further. "How about Wednesday at eight? I don't have a show, so the whole night would just be me and you."

"That works."

Ryan grinned. He couldn't control himself, and he pulled Jack into a kiss. Warmth blossomed in his stomach, spread up to his chest, and fuck if he wasn't getting horny again. He wanted to reward Jack, so he reached down and grabbed a handful. Jack moaned against his lips.

"You know what to do," Jack growled. Ryan did, so he dropped to his knees for the second time that day and pulled Jack free.

Jack came slower that go round, so Ryan had time to let himself have fun; when they were done, his lips were swollen, but both men were satisfied.

It didn't take Ryan long to get cleaned up and out of drag, and when he walked back into his bedroom, Jack was lying back on the bed, hands behind his head. Ryan flipped on the TV and flopped down next to him.

"This is the second performer found and though police are withholding further details, concerned citizens are beginning to wonder if these performers are being targeted."

Heart in his stomach, Ryan fumbled with the remote and clicked the Rewind button until the Breaking News banner flashed across the screen.

"Details are still coming in, but the body of a second drag performer has been found."

"No," Ryan whispered. This couldn't be happening. Not again.

A picture of a man flashed across the screen, and Ryan had to swallow the vomit rising in his throat.

"Thirty-six-year-old Jason Ramos performed as Taylor Maid several nights a week in various clubs around the city, according to a source close to the deceased. His body was found in an alley with his throat slashed, similar to victim Valentine Heartbreak, who was discovered a few weeks ago."

Ryan didn't hear the rest of the report. He clamored for breath, but couldn't draw any. There was no air left in the room. This was it. This was how it ended. He wouldn't have to worry about being gutted by some psycho, because his bed would be his grave. The room grew darker around him. The air was getting thin.

Next thing he knew, he was staring up at Jack, whose horrified expression chilled his blood.

"Are you okay?" Jack asked.

"No," Ryan said, trying to sit up, but Jack held him in place. "Another one of my friends is dead, so no, I am absolutely not okay."

"That's not how I meant it. I know you're not *okay* okay." Jack scrubbed a hand over his face. "But you passed out and rolled off the bed. Pretty sure you hit the floor headfirst, so I was trying to make sure you didn't crack your fucking skull open."

"Oh." Ryan moved to touch his head but stopped halfway. He couldn't remember anyone showing him that kind of affection before. To some it might have seemed minor, but to Ryan it was a big deal. "Yeah, I . . . I think I'm fine, thanks." He felt around to make sure there were no bruises or sore spots. He didn't seem to have any head injuries.

Jack didn't look all that convinced, but he helped Ryan up and back onto the bed.

"How long was I out?"

Jack shook his head. "It was only a few seconds, but you freaked me out. Maybe you should see a doctor?"

Ryan took a deep, shuddering breath. "I should be fine. Besides, I don't want to go anywhere right now." He stared up at the screen where the anchor droned on about some bill that was never going to pass, like someone hadn't just lost their life. Like another of Ryan's friends hadn't been brutally murdered.

It was official. Someone was after them. And nothing scared Ryan more than the thought of leaving the house and being the next victim. He couldn't stay here forever, though. There were bills to pay and shows to do, and Sheila was never one to disappoint her fans. But at least for today he would hide. Because here he was safe. Here he was with Jack.

As if Jack had heard his thoughts, he pulled Ryan into an embrace. "I know that there's nothing I can say. But I'm here for you."

That was all Ryan needed to know.

CHAPTER SEVEN

Jack pulled away from the curb after Taylor's funeral, glancing in Sheila's direction every minute or so. It had been nearly two weeks since they'd found Taylor's body, and Sheila hadn't been herself at all. He'd never known her to be so quiet before, but he understood why, and it made his chest ache.

Jack couldn't deny that he was falling in love anymore. The thought terrified him. Part of him wanted to take Ryan's hand and walk out into the world, fresh and new and officially dating instead of just fucking a few times a week. He found comfort in that idea. Warmth. Solace. But then there was that other, more cynical half that made him want to tuck his tail between his legs and get as far away from the situation as he could. Because it could only end in disaster for him. Heartbreak. Unemployment. His family disowning him the second they found out . . .

But it wasn't Jack's feelings that mattered right now.

This had been Taylor's second funeral. The first had been for Jason, held by his family, and they'd made it clear that none of his "drag friends" were welcome. So the queens had put together their own. A celebration of Taylor's life that they'd all showed up to completely decked out in their best drag. It had been a party—a send-off worthy of such a beautiful queen, they'd said. But now that it was over, Sheila looked like she wanted to sink back into the seat and disappear.

Jack cleared his throat. "How're you holding up?"

She was silent for a moment, visibly chewing her tongue. She glanced at Jack, eyes shimmering. "I don't know. Two of my sisters are dead. Murdered. And nobody—" Her voice broke and she heaved a sigh. "Nobody knows who did it, or why. And I've never been so scared in my life." She fixed her gaze on something out the window. "What if somebody really is targeting us? What if I'm next?"

"No," Jack said, putting his hand on her knee and squeezing in what he hoped would be a comforting way. "We're not going to let that happen."

Sheila scoffed. "And how do you think you can stop it? If some psycho decides he wants me dead, what is either one of us going to be able to do about it?"

"We can fight." Jack swallowed the emotion in his throat. "I don't want you giving up, so damn it, we're going to fight."

The corner of Sheila's mouth turned up in a half-hearted smile. "Careful, sugar. You're starting to sound like more than just a fuck buddy."

Jack rolled his eyes. Yeah, he wanted to be more. But every time he tried to say it, the words froze in his throat and he sat there, feeling like a coward. Because that's what he was. A giant pussy.

So they fell into silence, and stayed that way the rest of the ride back to Jack's apartment. As soon as they went inside, Sheila headed straight for the mini-drag closet Jack had set up for her, though normally she rarely used it. A few minutes later, Ryan walked into Jack's room, pulling a shirt on over his head.

"Thank you," he said.

"For what?"

"For coming with me today. I can't tell you how much it meant to me."

Jack nodded. "Of course I came with you. I wouldn't leave you to deal with something like this on your own."

Ryan stared at him for a long time, as if he was trying to figure something out. Jack rolled his shoulders and trained his gaze on a corner of carpet. He scooched over to make room for Ryan.

"Sorry," Ryan said. "I just . . ."

"Just what?"

"Nothing." He sat down on the bed, rested his head on Jack's shoulder. "I'm kinda in the mood for something sweet. What about you?"

Jack shrugged. "I've got some cake mix I've been needing to get rid of before it goes bad. I can whip that up, if you want."

"I didn't know cake mix went bad."

"Oh it does," Jack said, chuckling. "It can go real bad, and then everyone around pays the price." He remembered damn near poisoning his family at one of his sister's birthday parties and, in between heaves over the toilet, his sister grunting, *This is why men aren't supposed to try to cook.*

He shook the memory away. "You want that?"

"As long as it's not double chocolate," Ryan said.

"Understood. You gonna hang out here til I'm done?" Ryan nodded. Jack got up and padded off toward the kitchen.

He'd wanted to be a cook, growing up. But his family never approved of the idea. They discouraged him every chance they got and, eventually he gave up on that dream and went to law school. But the passion had never really left him. Even now as he mixed the ingredients, a calm that he hadn't felt in weeks rolled over him. Suddenly things made sense. Cases he'd been trying to figure out, and what to get his mother for her birthday, and, perhaps most importantly, what to do about Ryan.

He could do this. He could do a relationship, and it would be fine. He was a grown man, for crying out loud. What his family thought didn't mean shit. They weren't the ones who would have to live with the decision. He was. Being around Ryan made him happy. And if they really cared anything about Jack, they wouldn't try to take that away from him, regardless of how they felt about what did or didn't hang between Ryan's legs.

By the time he slid the cake pans in the oven, he'd decided that he was going to march into that bedroom with his head held high, kiss Ryan's breath away, fuck his brains out (not in drag, because that was the most important part), and tell him that he wanted to be in a relationship. That he was finally ready. He smiled the entire way down the hall, heart fluttering and skin tingling. And then he saw Ryan's face grinning up at him, hair disheveled and eyes twinkling like a man who was honest to God in love. Who wasn't afraid to take the next step because he wasn't a coward.

Jack lost all his nerve and, if he didn't know better, he would have sworn he felt his hopes crashing to the floor. Every time he'd ever heard his parents call someone a faggot, or a dyke, or a tranny swirled around in his head. The hatred in their eyes filled his brain. Each time they'd promised him that if he ever turned out like one of those limp-wristed fairies that he might as well just kill himself because he'd be dead to them came rushing back to him. He steadied himself against the doorway to keep from being knocked over by the wave of sorrow and disgust he suddenly found himself drowning in.

"Everything okay?" Ryan asked.

Jack swallowed. His gut told him to be honest, to give Ryan the chance to get out now, if that was what he wanted, because at this point Jack doubted he would ever be ready to give Ryan what he wanted and deserved. But when he opened his mouth, the only thing that came out was a lie. "Yeah. Yeah, I'm fine." He gave Ryan a half-hearted smile. "The cake will be done soon. It's strawberry." And he turned around and went back to the living room.

You're a fucking pussy, he scolded himself. But he could tell himself the same thing for the next fifteen years and it probably wouldn't change a damn thing. Because it was who he was. And that was one more thing his parents had beaten into his head every chance they got.

Pussies didn't win.

Ryan couldn't focus. His eyes slid over the statement of his client, Lillie, for what felt like the millionth time, but if anyone had asked him what it said, he'd be left staring at them, dumb. His mind kept floating back to Jack and the weirdness of whatever the fuck it was they had going on. It was definitely something *like* a relationship, but it was still in the super delicate phase where anything could break it. The problem was that the thing most likely to break it was the thing Ryan loved the most.

Jack still begged for more time whenever Ryan brought the subject up, but time, and Ryan's patience, were running razor thin. He hoped their upcoming date—a do-over from the originally planned one— would thaw the ice and make things a little better, but he was old enough to not hold out too much hope. People didn't change that much. They just grew further into who they really were.

Ryan snapped himself back to reality. The only thing he was supposed to be thinking about now was his client and how to win her case. He tried, once again, to read the paper in his hands, but three lines in he gave up. What was wrong with him?

He got up and paced his office, running a hand through his hair. This was exactly why he should have turned Jack away when he'd seen him coming toward the stage that night. Workplace trysts always got messy, and Ryan knew better. But he hadn't turned him away. And if he could go back in time, he probably still wouldn't have. Because the sex was fiery and their connection definitely grew more electric by the day. And it would keep getting more intense unless Ryan did something about it.

A knock on his doorframe brought him back to his senses. Jack stood there, looking all boyish and charming and damn if a blanket of calm didn't envelope Ryan and chase away the anxiety that had been plaguing him for the past hour.

"Everything okay?" Jack asked, head tilted to the side, studying him.

"Yeah, everything's fine. Just needed to stretch my legs."

Oh way to go, his brain scolded him. *Can't even be honest with him. How do you expect this to go anywhere when you won't tell the truth?*

Jack didn't appear convinced, but thankfully he didn't press the issue. "I finished drafting that complaint," he said. "I was hoping you'd give it a once-over for me."

"Sure thing."

"Great." He handed Ryan the folder and if Ryan didn't know any better, he'd have sworn a current passed through them before Jack let go. "And um . . ." Jack leaned in a little closer. "I'm really looking forward to tonight."

He turned around and took off up the hall before Ryan could try to read his expression. And there it was again. That niggling of unease that started in the pit of his stomach and would soon be buzzing through his entire soul. He pushed it to the side as best he could, because right now, work was more important.

At least, that's what he kept telling himself.

CHAPTER EIGHT

J ack took off another shirt and flung it across the room. Nothing looked right on him. And what was worse, it didn't usually take him this long to get ready for *anything*, much less to go out on a date that he definitely wanted to go on, no matter what that little voice in the back of his mind tried to tell him.

He stared at himself in the mirror. "What do you see in me?"

He must like me for me, the voice's hopeful counterpart supplied, overpowering the negative one for a quarter second.

"But what is there to like about me?" He shook his head and went back to his closet. It took him nearly half an hour to pick out something that didn't make him want to set it on fire, and by then he was sweating so bad he headed off for the shower again.

Nothing could go wrong tonight, because he still wasn't prepared to tell Ryan he could kick the drag to the curb. But he also didn't want to give him up. And even though he was feeling pressured to move faster than he was ready for—a pressure that would have had him giving any other relationship the boot—he had this inkling in his gut that this one might actually be worth it. So he would see where it went. And he'd move as fast as he could to make sure Ryan didn't go running.

An hour later, he was finishing buttoning his shirt when the phone rang. His heart sank into his stomach. His mother's face staring up at him was literally the last thing he needed right now, but he couldn't ignore her. She didn't call often and it might be important.

"Hey, Ma," he said, hoping he sounded happier than he felt.

"Hello, darling," she said, and it was clear she'd been drinking. All hopes for a decent conversation went out the window and he sank onto his bed.

"How's it going?"

"Oh, it's so kind of you to ask," she said. "It's only been a month since the last time you called me."

Fuck. Starting in already. He braced himself. "Sorry, Ma, I've just been crazy busy with work and—"

Her laugh cut him off. "I'm only fucking with you."

He blinked. "Say what?"

"I know you're busy. I wanted to check in on my baby and make sure you were still alive."

A smile pulled at the corner of his mouth. "Yeah, I'm still alive. Just buried under a really big case."

"Are you remembering to eat?"

His mind flashed back to a couple of days ago with his face buried between Ryan's cheeks. "Yes, I definitely am," he said, fighting a smirk.

They talked for the better part of an hour, catching up, and she made him promise to come visit before the holidays. He finished getting ready while they were on the phone, slipping into his pants at last, finding a decent pair of shoes, and spritzing himself with enough cologne to turn heads, but not enough to gag everyone in the room. The only person he wanted to lose their breath tonight was Ryan.

He'd almost forgotten why he didn't talk to his family back home, until he tried to get off the phone.

"Hey, it's been great, but I actually have to go. I have a date in a little bit and I've gotta get there."

"A date?" she asked, and the surprise in her voice made him regret his words. "I can't remember the last time you told me you had one of those. Is she a nice girl?"

He froze, mouth hanging open. Part of him wanted to tell her the truth, that he was going out with a man who was a drag queen who he was catching serious feelings for.

But the other part—the part that still needed her to love him no matter what—was scared shitless and couldn't handle the disgust he'd hear in her voice if he said anything like that. Or the disappointment in her eyes the next time he saw her—if he'd ever be allowed to see her again. The thought of never seeing his parents again pierced his heart like a dagger. So he swallowed the lump in his throat and kept that bit of info to himself.

"Yeah, she is. Really nice." It wasn't a lie. Not exactly.

"So now you definitely have to come for a visit. I can't wait to meet her." The pride there made him hate himself, and all of a sudden he was back to asking himself what Ryan even saw in him. "But you go on. Have fun tonight. I love you, honey."

"I love you too, Ma." He hoped she didn't hear the way his voice broke on the last word, and hung up before she could question him about it. Wiping away a tear, he tucked the phone into his pocket.

Just like that, he was back in his childhood room, sixteen, and wanting to kill himself because he'd rather die than lose the approval of those closest to him. His family had been all he'd had growing up. And now here he was, trying to make room in his heart for someone else; someone they would never approve of because they were stuck in the fifties. In their minds, there was no place for people like Jack— let alone people like Ryan—in the world. If the couple was anything other than a man and a woman, line up the firing squad and put them in front of it.

But Jack was sick of being unhappy. Sure, he could spend the rest of his life with a woman. And maybe he'd even turn out happy about it. But right now, in this moment, the one person he wanted to spend his time and energy on was probably in a car on the way to the restaurant to meet him, all put together and sexy. Jack nodded to himself. Ryan was who he needed to focus on now, and he couldn't let his family's outdated beliefs hold him back. So he put on a jacket and started out, head held high.

He wasn't so sure of himself by the time he was staring at the door of Emerald City, though. His heart pounded in his throat, the only thing keeping the vomit down. He'd already sweated though his shirt and it was all he could do not to turn heel and run. But when would he stop? No matter how far he went, from Ryan, the firm, his family, and the life he'd so carefully built . . . he couldn't run away from himself. And that grim outlook carried him inside and to the table where Ryan was already sitting.

Ryan stood. His smile was so radiant his eyes sparkled with it, and a sense of something like relief spread down Jack's spine. "Sorry I'm late," he said. "Traffic was a nightmare."

"It's fine," Ryan said, sitting back down. "Gave me time to dream up a new number for Sheila."

"Oh really?" Jack started to take off his jacket, remembered there were probably sweat stains on the pits of his shirt, and thought better of it. "What kind?"

Ryan launched into an explanation of the routine he'd been sketching in his brain for the past ten minutes: a Christina Aguilera song with tons of sparkles, but Jack was only half paying attention. His mind had drifted back to the conversation with his mother, and it was bringing him down again. It was impossible for her to walk in right now and find him sitting here with Ryan, ordering appetizers like a zombie, he knew that. But his brain had turned on him, and he found his gaze darting toward the door every few seconds to make sure they didn't have any unwelcome visitors.

"Do you have somewhere else you need to be?" Ryan asked, not bothering to hide the annoyance in his voice. "Cuz you know, I have better things I could be doing than sitting here being ignored." He shook his head. "You agreed to this. I didn't twist your arm."

The waiter chose that moment to show up with their drinks. "Here you are, gentlemen," he said, swooping down with the grace of a swan. It was kind of weird. Jack had never seen anyone move like that other than dancers. "One beer for you," he said, pushing a smoking bottle toward Jack. "And— Oh fuck! I'm so sorry!"

In all his grace, the waiter had dumped Ryan's drink right into his lap. Ryan shot up, grabbing a napkin from the table and dabbing at his crotch.

Part of Jack was mortified. Literally the only thing worse would have been Ryan leaving because Jack was such a douchebag. But another, filthier part came forward and seized the opportunity.

"Damn, babe, we haven't even finished dinner yet. I didn't think you'd be that wet already. Should I go ahead and get the check?" A long shot, but he had to take it or the evening would be over before it started.

Anger flashed in Ryan's eyes for a second, and then his lips split in a grin. "Hey, fuck you, all right? It's fucking cold." But he couldn't keep the laughter out of his voice. The waiter had grabbed a cloth from his apron and was hovering awkwardly, clearly not sure whether he should reach for Ryan's lap and help with the cleanup.

"It's fine," Ryan said, rubbing at his pants a few more times.

The dick-print showing through those tight slacks had Jack biting his tongue. For the first time in a long time, he could see himself on his knees, a cock in his mouth. Would he like it as much as he hoped? Only one way to find out, but he didn't think he was there yet.

"If you could just bring me some more napkins, please?" Ryan said. "That'd be great."

The waiter nodded and dashed off.

"You okay?" Jack asked as Ryan wiped up the wine that had spilled onto his seat.

"Yeah. Just not the greatest start to the night, you know?"

"Sorry." Jack wasn't certain which part he was apologizing for. He couldn't promise he'd be able to stay out of his own head and enjoy the moment, and if he couldn't, then they'd be right back where they were before the clumsy waiter.

But by the time their main course arrived (with Ryan's comped because of the wine mishap) the two of them had fallen into an easy conversation. Jack told Ryan about the phone call with his mother, and Ryan talked about how his family would always wake him up at the crack of dawn until he'd moved out because they were convinced that sleeping past 5 a.m. stunted your growth.

"I've never heard of anything like that." Jack snickered, stuffing his mouth full of chicken.

"Yeah, my family was crazy. It's not even like they had anything for me to do— they just honestly believed that. Probably still do. So I studied my ass off before school started. Part of why I became a lawyer. There were some times I really wanted to know if I could sue the pants off them."

"But what would you have gotten out of that?"

"I was twelve! I wasn't thinking that far ahead!"

Jack wiped his mouth to hide another laugh. "Okay. You win."

"But what was worse was my brother. He actually believes them. He's only a little over five feet, and he thinks it's because they let him sleep too long when he was a baby. He blames them for everything."

"Oh no," Jack said, downing the rest of his glass.

"Yeah. I love their crazy asses, though. I don't know what I'd do without them."

Jack knew that feeling. But his still came with the risk of denying who he was. He was questioning more and more if that was worth it.

He paid the check and they started toward the door, but Ryan stopped before they made it more than halfway. "Holy shit."

Jack turned and looked back at him. "What is it? What's wrong?"

"My brother."

Jack followed Ryan's gaze to the stout man standing just inside the door, clearly trying to get a table. He could see the family resemblance, the high cheekbones, tiny nose, thick lips. But Ryan's brother was a little thicker around the middle and definitely no slave to fashion. His clothes were oversized and dull. Jack glanced at his date again, how his entire outfit looked like it had been tailored to fit him, the warm-peach polo shirt, the bright-blue pants. Ryan was a man who knew his colors. His brother seemed to be the exact opposite.

"Mike?" Ryan called. "Mike, is that you?"

Mike turned in their direction, shock, then excitement registering on his face. "Rainey!" He came around the host's stand and made a beeline for them.

"What did he call you?" Jack asked out of the corner of his mouth.

Ryan didn't answer. It was too late to press him further because Mike was already on them, throwing his arms around his brother.

"How the hell have you been?"

"Fine," Ryan said, but something about his voice sounded off. Jack turned around and tried not to laugh. A perfect portrait of family awkwardness played out in front of his eyes. Ryan scratched at his head, his expression mortified. Mike, on the other hand, sported a huge grin, apparently ignorant to how bothered his brother seemed.

"I haven't heard from you in weeks, Rainey. Where have you been?"

Ryan closed his eyes as though calming himself. "Please stop calling me that."

"What is that?" Jack asked.

Mike turned toward him, eyebrow raised. "He with you?" he asked Ryan.

"Yeah. Sorry, this is—"

"Jack," Jack said, holding out his hand. Mike shook it, but he didn't look like he trusted Jack at all. It was odd, and a tendril of unease snaked its way down Jack's spine, but he shook it off. "Mike, was it? It's nice to meet you."

"You too." But Mike didn't seem like he meant it.

Jack turned back to Ryan. "So yeah. What's that all about, *Rainey*?"

Ryan cringed and Jack knew there was a story worth hearing behind it. "Nothing. Nothing at all. Can we go, please?"

"No way. Not until you have a drink with your little brother," Mike insisted.

"I'm down for that," Jack said.

Mike chewed the inside of his cheek. "Not to be rude . . ."

Jack braced himself. That statement was almost always followed by something that made him want to punch someone in the face.

"Then don't be," Ryan said. "Mom and Dad aren't here. You don't have to act like a brat." He clapped his brother on the shoulder and let out a laugh, but it was clearly fake. The air around them was suddenly super uncomfortable, and Jack wanted nothing more than to get the fuck out of there before anything got worse.

"I was only going to ask what you guys had been doing before I got here, Rainey. Wasn't trying to be nasty."

Ryan narrowed his gaze, but nodded. "We were just having some dinner."

There was that eyebrow again. Any higher and it was going to get lost in that mane of hair. "This a client of yours? Did I interrupt you prepping for a case?"

"No, nothing like that." Ryan bit his bottom lip, a war playing out on his face, before saying, "Jack is just—"

"We were on a date," Jack said. The word tasted funny, like it hadn't been cooked all the way through. And he found himself scanning the restaurant, making sure there weren't any of *his* family members lurking in the shadows.

Ryan's mouth fell open, and Mike raised an eyebrow, apparently impressed. Jack's face was on fire, but he fought it back, because the excitement spreading over Ryan's face was enough to suppress his own discomfort.

"You didn't tell me you had a boyfriend, bro."

"That's because I don't," Ryan said, though he cast a sidelong glance at Jack as if for confirmation. "We're just trying things out."

Mike swept his gaze over Jack again, as though sizing him up for the first time. "Come join us, then." And he grabbed Ryan and frog marched him over to the bar.

Jack followed, dodging the daggers Ryan shot at him with his eyes. He pulled up a stool and ordered a whiskey sour and an incredible hulk.

"Really, Mike, we've gotta go."

"One drink won't kill you." Mike looked at the cup the bartender put down. "Well, that one might," he said. "It's pretty strong. You'll never know what hit you."

Ryan gave a defeated sigh. He sipped the green concoction the bartender had slid in front of him and winced.

"No one ever told me what this Rainey thing is all about," Jack said.

Ryan's expression soured and, for a second, Jack wondered if he was about to throw his drink in Jack's face.

Mike laughed. "Okay, so when we were younger, Ryan here used to say that everyone drove him crazy and the only time he could find peace was when it rained outside. Cuz no one else was around, you know? So every time it rained, he would go outside and just sit in it. I can't tell you how many times he got sick from doing that dumb shit."

"That's enough," Ryan said. "It was a long time ago. I know better now."

"You did it the night before your high school graduation."

"There were fifty people in the house! What was I supposed to do, sit there with them talking at me about what I was going to do with my future?"

Mike turned to Jack. "It was a hundred degrees outside. My parents had the AC blasting in the house and his dumbass caught the flu."

Ryan shrugged. "Kept everyone away, didn't it?"

"But they still made him go to the ceremony the next day, because everyone had come to town for it. Got half the class sick."

Ryan almost looked ashamed. "That wasn't supposed to happen."

Mike clapped him on the shoulder. "It was years ago. Everyone is fine now."

"And yet you still brought it up." Ryan downed the rest of his drink. He stood up. "It was really great to see you, Mike, but we've gotta get going. I'll call you, okay?"

Without waiting for a response, he turned and headed for the door. Jack was confused, but a cue was a cue, so he shook Mike's hand and followed Ryan outside. He found him at the corner, forehead pressed against the brick.

"Hey, what's up?"

Ryan looked at him, eyes sparkling. He was silent for a long time, and then said, "Remember when I said my parents thought that sleeping past five stunted your growth?"

"Yeah."

"Well, before I realized how batshit they were, I believed them. Why would they lie to me, you know?" Jack nodded. Ryan wiped a tear away. "I overslept a lot when I was a kid. And for a while, I was scared they were right. So I started sneaking my mother's heels. Just so I'd know how to walk in them when I wound up short. And then one day my dad caught me in them." He turned around, slid down the wall. "He beat the shit out of me." Ryan cried freely now, head cradled in his hand. "Having a gay son was one thing. He could deal with that, he said. But no way was he raising a cross-dressing nancy-boy. He'd die first." Ryan let out a bitter bark of a laugh. "If only dear old Dad could see me now."

Jack hoped he was doing a good job of hiding his disgust. His own parents had been shitty, yeah, but he couldn't imagine being accepted for being gay, only to be looked down on doing drag.

Ryan looked back at Jack. "That's why I spent so much time trying to get away from them as I got older, even if it meant going and sitting out in the rain. I liked how I felt wearing the heels. And I wanted to do more. But I didn't trust him anymore. I dunno, I guess I thought he'd be able to see on my face how much I wanted to dress up, or something. So I kept my distance. It was safer that way. At least in my mind."

Jack pulled Ryan to his feet and embraced him.

"No one ever knew," Ryan whispered.

"I'm sorry," Jack said. "We should have left when you first wanted to. I've just been fucking up all over the place tonight."

"It's not your fault," Ryan said. "I thought I was past this, but I guess I'm not."

"It made you into who you are."

"Some broke-down drag queen who has to play lawyer during the day because she can't make a living doing what she really loves?"

"Hey." Jack put himself in Ryan's field of vision so he was looking him in the eye. "You are not broke-down. You're as good as any of the other bitches out there doing it full-time, if not better, and you know it." He used his thumb to wipe away one of Ryan's tears. "We've all got fucked-up pasts. But we got away. We're winning."

Ryan clearly thought he was full of shit, but faked a smile anyway. "Thank you."

"Nothing to thank me for. All I'm doing is telling you the truth." He took Ryan's hand in his own. "Let's get back."

"Where?"

"Doesn't matter. My place or yours." He led Ryan across the street. "We can watch TV. I could fuck you. Maybe I could kick your ass in Monopoly. It's up to you. Anything you want."

Jack preferred the second option, but he wouldn't push it. They had both been emotional in the last few hours, so the night was about healing. There was always time for more sex, and Jack couldn't think of anyone he'd rather have it with than Ryan.

So why was his mind already rifling through the closet, picking out looks for Sheila?

INTERLUDE UNKNOWN

I walked into the club, taking a quick moment to scan the room and make sure I'd stay inconspicuous. Hundreds of people and I didn't recognize a single one of them. Perfect.

I sized up the crowd as I passed them. I wouldn't be able to take down most of these guys, even on their worst days. Some of them I could probably overpower without too much trouble, but they weren't why I was here. The main attraction would show themselves before long. In the meantime, I slid up to the bar and ordered a whiskey. None of those *namby-pamby* drinks for me. I'm a man, and I drink like one.

Being around all the shirtless, dancing men didn't repulse me as much as it had the first time I'd visited a place like this. I might even be getting used to it. I downed my liquor and ordered another before moving closer to the stage. Tonight's performer was still a mystery to me, but tonight was the last night they'd be alive. I promised myself that.

I reached into my pocket and fingered the handle of my knife, just to be certain one more time that I hadn't forgotten it, because then the whole trip would have been for nothing. I smiled to myself and swayed to the music until the show started.

As soon as the voice came over the speaker and announced that tonight's victim would be some bitch called Sheila, I let myself be swallowed by the crowd. The key to being a good serial killer was to never look too suspicious, and a man by himself in a club like this, hovering around the stage was definitely suspect.

When Sheila (or whatever *his* real name was) stepped out, the crowd erupted. Clearly, the man had fans. People who would be devastated when the body was found, and that made what I was planning that much sweeter. They'd never know I'd been among them. Watching. Waiting. Using them as my shadow and wall.

The man on stage wore a sparkling silver gown with one sleeve and a brunette wig pulled back into a tight bun. The blood-red lipstick was a stark contrast to the rest of the look and was even more pronounced when the lights went down and a single spotlight shone onto him.

All in all, it would have been beautiful on a real woman.

A somber expression graced Sheila's face as he surveyed the audience. A piano started in low over the speaker, framing an obvious ballad and, a moment later, the man on stage started to fake it.

"What you gave me, I know you gave me . . . You remind me all the time."

I knew that voice. Christina something. Addison? Austin? Aguilar? I remembered that one song about the genie, but forced the thought away. It didn't matter who the singer was. Nothing mattered except my plan.

But I wondered what had inspired the queen to perform this of all songs. The lyrics were a dark, heartbreaking story of love gone wrong. A woman, falling in love with a man who wasn't right for her, walking on eggshells and trying everything she could to keep him happy, even at the risk of losing herself. Halfway through, as the bridge built and built to what must be the real power of the end of the number, I thought I saw tears in the performer's eyes. And then the man on stage was definitely crying, microphone in hand, performing as though he was really pouring his heart out for everyone to see. Who had hurt this poor son of a bitch? I might ask before I put him out of his misery, but I doubted it.

When the number ended, applause erupted all over the club. It went on for nearly a full minute before Sheila announced a short break and disappeared from the stage, dabbing at his eyes with a tissue he'd pulled from his fake tit. I debated making my move now, but that would be too risky. People were expecting the show to go on and, if the main attraction didn't come back, people would get suspicious. So I'd wait. I wasn't in any rush.

Two more glasses later, my head was getting foggy. Who had I come here to kill? What was their name? Something about the music made me want to move. I'd never liked dancing, but whatever this song was seemed to be rewiring me. I moved with the beat, all but forgetting my mission and, before long, a stout man with adoration in his eyes sidled up to me and closed the space between us. The fairy was bare-chested, covered in glitter, and grinding his ass into a total stranger's crotch. Big mistake. But I didn't *want* to stop dancing. Especially when I finished the last of my cup and felt that familiar twitch as my dick came to life.

I closed my eyes, imagining a woman's ass pressed against me, because at least then I could keep my alcohol down. My head swam, and next thing I knew I was fully hard and the fleshy, denim-clad cheeks had been replaced with a hand. My first instinct was to snap. But this could be useful. I hadn't had a halfway decent blowjob in ages and, when I opened my eyes, I found the queer staring up at me, bottom lip caught between his teeth. Swallowing my disgust and throwing caution to the wind, I let myself be led off the floor and toward a couple of doors bathed in red light.

They turned out to be bathrooms and, before I knew what was happening, I was being shoved into a stall in the men's room and, the faggot was pulling down my pants, freeing my cock and sinking to the ground.

Fuck it was nice to have someone's mouth on me again, even if it was . . . I couldn't bring myself to think it, so I submitted to the intoxication and let myself enjoy the ride. I'd already decided how it was going to end, so why ruin what might be the best orgasm of my life by thinking?

A couple of minutes later, my companion wasn't satisfied anymore with just a dick in his mouth. He pushed me down onto the toilet, freed himself of his own pants, slicked himself with spit, and hopped on.

Shit shit shit. This wasn't happening. I wasn't inside another man, but fuck if it wasn't tight and warm, and damn it I was already on the verge of climax. I didn't want this to be happening. But at the same time why shouldn't it? This didn't make me gay. Or anything like it. This loser had come on to *me*. Had basically been molesting me since we'd been on the dance floor. And now he was riding me. Because that's what he'd decided to do. I was the real victim here.

I couldn't think anymore. The ass felt too good, but I had to act fast. So I waited a few seconds more, until I wouldn't be able to hold back much longer. I was there, on the verge of ecstasy. My balls tightened. My muscles starting to seize, so with my last of ounce of clarity as I tumbled over the edge into utter bliss, I reached up, put a hand on either side of his head and wrenched until the neck snapped. Stars exploded in my vision as he went limp and fell back against me. It could only have been a few seconds that I sat there, panting harshly in the suddenly silent room, but it could have just as easily been an hour. Especially once I realized what I'd done.

Fucking him had been bad enough, but I could live with that. But I'd shot my load in him. And I wasn't wearing a condom. How could I have been so stupid? I'd have to physically get rid of the body.

But how was I supposed to get it out of here without being seen?

CHAPTER NINE

"**A**uthorities are continuing to search for Simon Hall, who has now been missing for approximately three weeks. Today, his family issued a new statement and are offering a reward for any information leading to his safe return." The camera switched from the newscaster to two women and a man standing in front of blue and green house. One of the women, an older lady with patches of gray in her auburn hair, seemed to be crying.

Ryan couldn't watch this. He switched off the television and got up. Simon had come to Neon Trees a few times to see Sheila perform. They'd talked, and Simon had gushed over how much he loved her numbers. Ryan felt sick that he was missing. He tried to ignore the obvious fear that Simon had become the newest victim of the lunatic stalking the city. But Simon didn't do drag, that Ryan knew of. So he should have been safe . . . right?

Ryan shoved the thought away. This wasn't the same. No body had been found. Which wasn't necessarily a great thing, but this didn't match the killer's MO. On top of that . . . Ryan couldn't handle wondering if they'd both been in the club, watching him. And that a different man had maybe gotten a fate meant for him. The only victims up until now had been drag queens, so Sheila being the next target wasn't a nonsensical jump. Chewing the inside of his cheek, Ryan paced the living room for ages, but he eventually forced himself to pick up his phone.

Jack answered on the second ring.

"I was just about to call you."

"Oh really?"

"Yeah. I was gonna see if you wanted to catch a movie, or something."

Ryan toyed with that for a moment. But he wasn't sure if he was up for leaving. Maybe another night, but for now . . . "I kinda wanted to stay in. I was actually calling to see if you wanted to come over. We can watch something here."

"Sure thing. I'll be there in a bit."

"Great." Ryan hung up. But what to do until Jack arrived? Maybe he'd start planning his next number.

When the doorbell rang almost an hour later, Ryan was in his closet, staring at a pair of thigh-high red boots with a heel that would have scared the life out of him only a year ago. He smiled. If nothing else, hanging out with Jack had made him more adventurous. He filed away the act he'd been dreaming up for Sheila and went to let his guest in.

The grin Jack sported when Ryan opened the door took his breath away. "Hey," he said, stepping aside. He hoped his face wasn't as red as it felt.

Jack swooped in and kissed him. A small peck, but Ryan still froze, caught totally off guard. For half a second, he wanted to run to the bathroom, but then he remembered that this was what butterflies felt like. And now there was definitely warmth creeping up his neck, into his cheeks. He couldn't have hidden it if he'd wanted to.

"What was that for?" he asked, resisting the urge to touch his lips.

"I didn't know that I needed a reason."

"You don't," Ryan said quickly. "I just wasn't expecting it."

"Aren't those the best ones?"

Ryan knew the look in Jack's eyes. That hunger. It turned a small part of him on, but he wasn't in the mood for sex tonight. Peace was more important.

"Let's take a walk," Jack said, jerking his chin toward the steps as he shut the door.

A weight dropped onto Ryan's chest, but he still allowed himself to be led up the stairs and back into his drag closet. He tried to contain the annoyance bubbling inside him, but it grew larger, more intense, until he could practically taste it.

"What is this?" he asked as Jack pulled a red wig off its head and held it up against a corset.

"What do you mean?"

"I mean what we're doing," he said. It came out more biting than he'd intended, and Jack turned around.

Confusion colored his face. "What's wrong?"

"Well for starters," Ryan said, pointing at the hair hanging limply in Jack's hand. "That's a four-hundred-dollar wig and I just finished styling it last night."

Jack swallowed visibly and returned it to the foam head it had been sitting on. "And?"

Ryan sighed. "I'm not a woman."

"I know that—"

"But you'll only fuck me when I'm dressed like one."

"Ry—"

"You know? I didn't even call you over here for sex. I legit just needed a friend."

"Okay. I'm sorry. I didn't know."

"That's not even the point anymore." Anger burst in, shoving all his other emotions out of the way. "We've been fucking for almost four months. I told you weeks ago that I didn't like dressing in drag all the time, but you think it's okay to waltz into my house and start rifling through stuff for me to wear just so you can get off."

"That's not what I meant—"

"But it's what you did." His nails dug into the palm of his hand. He couldn't even remember making the fist, but now that he realized it, he had to keep himself from punching a hole through the wall. "It's what you always do. And you don't even give a damn how I feel about it."

"I do, I swear."

"You don't. Nobody ever does. I'm never good enough for anybody. I wasn't man enough for my father because I dressed up as a girl. I'm not enough for you because I'm not a woman."

"You are enough." Jack took a step toward him, but Ryan held up a hand to stop him and backed away. Jack threw his hands up in surrender. "I told you I just need a little more time."

"You said that two months ago. What are you waiting for? For me to die?"

"No, of course not." Jack scrubbed a hand over his face. "Everything was fine last night. Hell, everything was fine an hour ago when you called me over here. So why is this such a big issue right now?"

"Because I'm falling in love with you!"

The words left Ryan's mouth before he could stop them, and now that they were out in the world, there was no taking them back. Jack stood there, mouth hanging open. Obviously dumbstruck.

They were silent for nearly a minute before Jack whispered, "Please." He shook his head. "We don't have to have sex. I'm okay with that. I just ... I need a little more time. I promise you I'm getting there. That kiss back there? I've never felt a spark like that before. That's how I know."

Ryan knew what he meant. But it wasn't enough. He'd spent so much time ashamed of part of himself, and now that he'd come to accept everything, he wasn't about to let anyone shove him back into that box. He remembered the disgust in his father's eyes for days after he'd caught him in those heels. And the side-eyes people had given him when he'd first started doing drag because he wasn't as pretty as the other queens. How he'd hated himself for ever wanting to dress up in the first place. Now, in the one place he was supposed to be comfortable, those old insecurities were creeping back in, nibbling at the confidence it had taken him so long to build. He couldn't let that happen. Not for Jack. Not for anyone.

"I'm sorry, but I don't have any more time." Ryan fought back the tears. "Because one day, I'm going to realize that I don't want to spend my life with anyone but you. And that same day ..." He sniffled and took a deep, steadying breath. "You're going to tell me that you're leaving me because this isn't enough for you anymore and you'd rather have the real thing. And I just can't put myself through that."

"I swear to you ... I give you my word that will never happen."

"You're right. Because I'm not going to let it. So I need you to decide right now ... do you want Ryan? Or is it Sheila that you're really here for?"

"Y'all are the same person."

Ryan swallowed and let the first tear fall. "Wrong answer," he said in a shaky whisper. He chewed the corner of his top lip. Fuck, he didn't want to do this, but he had to. For himself. "Rhythm nation."

Jack looked confused for a moment, but then realization spread over him as he clearly recognized Ryan's safeword. The floodgates were open now, and there was no stopping the wave of emotion, but Ryan stood his ground.

"Please . . . don't do this."

"I, um, I think you should go."

Jack's bottom lip quivered. For a moment, he stared at Ryan with helpless, pleading eyes. But Ryan wouldn't budge. Jack swallowed. Nodded. Drew himself up to his full height. "Then please consider this my two weeks' notice. Because I can't work for you anymore."

Before Ryan could say a word, Jack tucked his head, squeezed past him and out into the hall.

Ryan waited until he heard the front door close, then he let out a watery breath and sank to his knees.

He sobbed until he thought he'd die.

CHAPTER TEN

Jack fingered the tube of lipstick in his pocket as he watched the door. He'd gone and picked up Ryan's favorite shade of red before he'd come here, still holding on to hope that Ryan might show. But now—two and a half hours into the worst birthday party of his life— he was *almost* convinced he'd wasted his time. But that small part of him Sheila had awakened refused to stop believing. Yeah, he'd fucked up. Royally. But Ryan wouldn't leave him hanging. Not today.

He gave the room a quick scan, in case Ryan had managed to sneak in without him noticing, but there was no sign of him. Jack ran a hand through his hair, ignoring the persistent gnawing in his gut. He fished his phone out of his other pocket, but the generic night sky background mocked him with its emptiness. He hated himself for falling so hard for his boss (*of all fucking people!*), because now the feelings refused to go away. For more than a week, everywhere he turned, memories rained down on him like plagues, attacking almost every waking moment.

He had no intentions of giving this up without a fight. He'd called a dozen times. Left voice mails. Sent texts. But to make matters worse, he hadn't gotten a single fucking response. He'd showed up at the club, only to be turned away by the bouncer. That had been when he'd decided to cool it before he got arrested for stalking. But then he'd seen Ryan in the office, and damn it, he'd just wanted to talk to him. So he'd cornered him in the bathroom, at first planning to ask him if he was still coming to the party. But Ryan hadn't been having it.

Ryan fixed him with an ice-cold stare. "If it's not about business," he said, "you don't have anything to say to me."

"But—"

"*But nothing. You've only got a few days left, and either you stay professional, or you're fired. And you know how fast word travels in the firms in this city.*"

Threatening his livelihood? How professional was that? Instinct told him since Ryan had taken the first stab, to cut back and cut deeper. Jack almost threatened him with exposure. But it would have just been anger talking. He wouldn't have meant it and would have regretted saying it for the rest of his life. Partly because it was a shitty thing to do, but mostly because he'd never get Ryan back if he did. Wounded, Jack bit his tongue. Throat suddenly dry, he swallowed and licked his lips. "*I just want to hold you,*" *he said, barely more than a whisper. If Ryan heard it, he pretended not to.*

"*So do you have anything business-related to discuss?*"

"*No, sir.*"

"*Then I guess you'd better get back to work.*"

And he was gone.

The rest of the day, Jack had only seen glimpses of him: rounding a corner here, closing a conference room door there.

What was he supposed to do? Let it all go and pretend like the best time of his life hadn't happened?

Fat fucking chance.

"Did someone shoot your dog or something?" a voice came from behind him. He turned to find his cousin standing there. He was a slender man with a mess of dirty-blond hair that looked like he hadn't taken a comb to it in about six years.

"I don't have a dog, Cal."

"So why are you standing here looking all sad and shit? It's your fucking birthday and you're bringing everyone down."

Jack scoffed. "No one's even paying attention to me. They probably don't even know I'm here."

"Oh stop acting like a little bitch whose boyfriend left her." That one got him. Right in the heart. "Everyone knows you're here. We all came out here for you."

He tried to fake an interested smile and failed. He scanned the crowd again, this time looking for anyone, even one person, looking in his direction.

Not even one.

He did see his mother, though, chatting up the bartender as he slid another martini her way. He shook his head. Flirting until you got what you wanted was the Kieza way. But that gene must have skipped him, because he'd never been any good at it. If he had, Ryan would be standing next to him, and they'd probably be deep in their own conversation and ignoring everyone else in the room.

Jack chewed the inside of his cheek. When Ryan was around, there was no one else. The world was just the two of them.

Fingers snapped in front of his face. "Hello? Earth to dipshit!" Jack turned his attention back to his cousin. "Are you listening to me?"

"Not really, no."

Cal's face went red and, for a moment, it looked like he might deck Jack. But instead he forced a grin and clapped Jack on the shoulder. "Watch yourself," he said. "It's not going to be your birthday much longer."

He gave Jack a warning look and disappeared into a crowd of people who Jack *might* have met before.

God, he didn't know most of the people here. Why had he agreed to come in the first place? Another peek at his mother as she swirled an olive in her glass reminded him. She'd been badgering him since his *last* birthday. Because *"You only turn thirty once."* He could hear her saying it so clearly that she might have been standing right next to him instead of across the room.

Biting his bottom lip, he checked his phone again. Still empty. He knew nothing was wrong with it, but rebooted it just in case. Sometimes he'd do that and get texts that hadn't made it through before. When nothing pinged, he cast one last longing glance at the door and, grudgingly, made his rounds.

He spent almost half an hour forcing laughter. Faking smiles. Same old tired thing he did at business dinners. He tried to focus on the things people said to him, but they might as well have been speaking another language.

Finally, he came to his immediate family.

"—punched his fucking face in." Laughter erupted from his sister, brother, and his parents as Cal mimed hitting someone.

He didn't know what he'd walked into, but already he was planning escape routes. He couldn't just pretend that he'd been walking past them. Maybe he could fake a bathroom emergency, though. Or act like his aunt Sasha had called to him; he'd spotted her across the room pouring whatever was in her glass into a plant. Cal's mother was by no means a saint, but Jack liked her better than the jackals he found himself next to now.

"That'll teach them," his father said. "Fucking faggots."

His mother's face was a mask of disgust. "I don't understand why a man would do that to himself. Being gay is bad enough, but why would you want to dress like a woman?"

"I bet he won't do that shit again." Cal's face twisted into a proud sneer, and then Jack really did need to make a bathroom run. His stomach churned, the taste in his mouth metallic. He had to choke down the vomit before he tossed it over everyone standing in front of him.

"What did you do?" he blurted before he could stop himself. His cousin had just admitted to beating someone he'd interpreted to be a man dressed like a woman, hadn't he? Cal had a temper on him, Jack knew that from childhood and the many run-ins with cops. Was it really that far a leap from beating someone to other, darker things? Jack's brain swam with pictures of men in dumpsters, throats slashed from ear to ear. But Cal wasn't capable of that? Was he?

Cal glared at him like he knew everything he'd been doing over the last few weeks. And with who.

"Some queer thought it would be a good idea to try his hand with me. Dressed up like a chick and thought I wouldn't notice. So I showed him what we do to freaks like him."

Jack shook his head. "Not all of us."

"Oh save the bleeding-heart shit for someone else," Cal said. "He got what was fucking coming to him for acting like that. You wanna get fucked in the ass and dress up and pretend you got a fucking pussy, then you do that shit behind closed doors where the rest of us God-fearing people can't see it. Cuz if you bring it in front of me, better believe I'm going to have something to say and do about it."

Jack knew that his cousin wasn't talking about him directly, but it felt like he was. There was no way he could have known about his bisexuality, though. Jack had made sure that the only person who knew anything about him wanting men was Ryan. And Jack was suddenly thankful that Ryan wasn't here. He wouldn't want him to hear this bullshit. But now, as another part that Ryan had awakened in him roared to life, Jack dug his nails into the palm of his hand. His face was on fire. "And who gives you that right?"

"I do. And my president. And the Good Book. All those faggot pieces of shit deserve to die."

"I hope he presses charges," Jack said. "I'll represent him for free."

If his mother had been wearing pearls, she would have been clutching them. They all stared at him like he'd sprouted a second head, but Cal actually took a step forward. "I always knew you were one of them," he said, looking Jack up and down. "Ever since I caught you looking at my dick when we were kids, I knew you'd take it up the ass one day."

"I wouldn't touch your dick if it were the last one on Earth. I'd just never seen one that small."

He realized half a second before Cal punched him that he'd kind of come out. But then his head snapped back and he stumbled. He caught himself and blocked the next one his cousin threw.

A red haze clouded the edges of Jack's vision. He landed a blow against Cal's cheek and, while Cal was dazed, aimed another at his throat, then his chest, then stomach. Cal hunched over and Jack seized the opportunity to introduce his knee to his cousin's nose. There was a snap of bone before blood sprayed all over the floor. His mother screamed, and he froze. What was he doing? He wasn't violent. He didn't even kill bugs when he saw them in the apartment. The sanity he hadn't even felt slipping away crept back in on him. Jack opened his mouth, not even sure what he wanted to say. Next thing he knew, hands were around his arms, dragging him backward. Cal stumbled to Sasha, cowering like a kid who needed to be protected from a monster. Didn't he, though? Jack certainly felt monstrous. But he remembered how they'd gotten there, why he'd snapped, and anger flared inside him all over again.

Jack wrenched himself free of his father and brother and straightened, smoothing his shirt. He looked at his cousin's bruised, bloody face, his stomach churning. "You'd better not *ever* let me hear you talking like that again. Because those—" He stopped for a second and considered what he was about to say. "—*us* faggots have more balls than you ever will."

There was utter silence in the room. It pressed in on him, almost deafening. He surveyed the people he'd grown up with; suddenly it hit home, if he never saw any of them again, he'd be perfectly fine with it.

"You all make me sick." He turned on his heel and strode away, head held high. Through the door to the ballroom. Out into the cooling night air and across the street. He couldn't believe what he'd done. But part of him swelled with pride he'd never known. After twenty-nine years, he'd stood up to the people who had made him hate himself and feel like he was less than the rest of them simply because of the way he was.

But he was something else now. Besides a bisexual man. Besides a man who'd fallen head over heels in love with a drag queen. Besides a probably now-disowned man from Brooklyn who'd craved nothing more growing up than the acceptance of the people he'd just alienated.

Finally, he was free.

CHAPTER ELEVEN

Sheila stared at herself in the mirror. Even under the makeup, she could see Ryan and how much pain he was in. The emotionless depths of his eyes. The droop of his lips underneath the ones she'd drawn on. Even the hunch of his shoulders.

She couldn't be her true, authentic self if both parts of her personality weren't on board. But Ryan couldn't go back and talk to Jack. Not now. Probably not ever. It would hurt too much. Because if Jack hadn't come to terms with himself by now, he likely never would, and Ryan couldn't deal with that. He wouldn't be thrust back into the closet like an old jacket, and that was the way he felt with Jack. Like he was hiding behind Sheila again. Yeah, Sheila was fabulous and took no shit, and she'd taught Ryan more about being a man than most men in his life, but he couldn't be her forever. Sometimes he had to come back to himself. No matter how much he hated being that person. Especially now.

It had killed him to be so mean to Jack, to watch his phone as it rang and just turn it over so he didn't have to see that beautiful face staring up at him, to threaten him the way he had. But Jack had to know he meant business. That Ryan was putting his foot down and enough was enough. It was time to put the persona away.

Sheila sighed and pulled at her wig; the bobby pins tugged at the hair they'd been secured to but gave way, and just like that, the illusion of the woman in the mirror had been shattered. Ryan looked from his boy hair down to his still fully beat face and was once again shocked by the difference. He was no one special. Had no real talents to speak of, so how had he created such a character and painted her so beautifully onto his face? Even after all this time, he still couldn't understand it.

Next, the lashes came off, then he slipped a wipe from the makeup remover container on his sink and started to scrub at his face. Layer after layer, Sheila disappeared further from the world until nothing was left except the body he'd crafted. Then it was the dress, the bra, the tights, the padding. He untucked, wincing only a little as he pulled the duct tape away faster than he'd meant to. His dick stung for a moment, but nothing he wasn't used to.

And he was Ryan again. He resisted the urge to cover himself. There was no one else in his house, but that didn't make him feel any less exposed. Like he'd revealed himself to the entire world for their jokes and criticisms. He was always fine when he put his boy clothes on, but he'd found that he needed moments like this, no matter how fleeting, to remind himself that underneath all the business suits and the sequins and hair, that he was still just the scared boy who had no idea what he was doing with his life.

He wished Jack could see him this way.

But the time for pitying himself was over. He put on a pair of sweats and a white T-shirt before he sat on his bed and turned on the TV.

Big mistake.

A Breaking News banner rolled across the bottom of the screen. KILLER STRIKES AGAIN? stood against the red background, and Ryan thought he was going to be sick. "The body of performer Dolly Mattell was found just moments ago in the alley behind me," the newswoman said, gesturing toward the usually empty space between Neon Trees and the pizza place next to it. Her face was like paper, eyes wide, and she seemed to be shaking her head back and forth as she spoke. The entrance to the alleyway was marked by police tape, and the alley itself was crawling with officers. He'd left there less than an hour ago. How had they gotten there so fast?

The reporter he knew, because she'd tried to get a comment out of Sheila as he'd been leaving. Ironically, she wanted to know if he thought he might be a target for the serial killer on the loose.

"I stepped away from the front door to have a cigarette, and that's when I discovered the grisly scene," the reporter said. "I was here, collecting interviews for WVOT, and so you're hearing here first that it would appear the killer has struck again."

This wasn't possible. Ryan had just finished a set with Dolly. She'd gone on first, did a few numbers with Sheila and then Sheila closed the show. She'd left early to get ready because she was supposed to be heading to her brother's wedding tomorrow.

The reporter kept talking, but Ryan didn't hear anything she said. What if she'd been right? Sheila was obviously a target because this bastard was only attacking drag queens. But what if she was next? What if whoever this was had been there, watching and waiting?

Ryan wasn't ready to die.

God, he wanted to call Jack. Ryan was pretty sure Jack would answer the phone, but he couldn't bring himself to do it, no matter how scared shitless he was. Jack hadn't tried to call or text him since Ryan had missed his birthday party. It had only been a day, but still, it didn't get much shitter than missing something like that and then calling because he needed to be comforted. Besides, after the things Ryan had said, he was surprised Jack had kept trying to get in touch with him at all.

But that seemed to be over. So he sat there. Alone.

He looked back at the TV in time to see Sidney, the club manager on screen. Tears streamed down his face and he looked like a breakdown was right around the corner. "Until this madman is captured," he was saying, "all drag-related activity at Neon Trees is suspended. Our top priority is the safety of our patrons and our performers. We're sorry it took us so long to come to this decision, but we were hoping he would have been apprehended by now."

Ryan's heart sank. So not only were his friends being murdered, but now he'd lost the one emotional outlet he had. He hated himself for even thinking that. It felt selfish, but it was honest. Without drag, he probably would have killed himself a long time ago.

Jack danced back into his mind, all sexy and wounded and . . . there. One relapse wouldn't hurt, would it? But Ryan needed more courage before he could make that call. So he padded down to the kitchen with the rational part of his mind trying to talk him out of his plan the whole way. It was no match for the raw loss, though, and a moment later Ryan plopped down on one of his stools, pried open a bottle of whiskey, and poured himself a cup.

The resolve he wanted wasn't at the bottom of that one, so he went for another. And another. By the end of the bottle, his head was wading into the deep end of the bad-decision pool. He stared at his phone, but still couldn't will himself to make the call. So he got up for another and toppled over. His head hit the ground and he winced, but refused to move yet. Maybe he belonged down here. He lay there, staring up at the ceiling and hating himself for wanting Jack so bad, but he couldn't help it. For the last few weeks, he'd shared literally every part of his life with him, and now he couldn't and it would have been less painful if he'd just jumped into a pool of acid.

Something chimed in the distance, and he rolled over and to his feet a little too fast. The room swam around him; he had to grab the island to steady himself. He reached for his phone, but it was blank. So what the hell had that been?

And there it was again. He looked around, eyes darting from one end of the kitchen to the other. Had he left music playing somewhere? Then came the banging, and Ryan realized what it was. He did have a doorbell. At least, he thought he did. So he stumbled through the living room and into the foyer as it chimed once more.

There was a shadow on the other side of the frosted glass. A Jack-shaped shadow. He staggered toward the door, elation flooding him, and threw it open—fuck him sideways Jack was really there, staring at him through grieving eyes.

"I'm so sorry," Jack whispered.

But apologies didn't matter. Not anymore. "Shut up and get in here." Ryan pulled him inside and into the kiss he'd been aching for for the past two weeks. Everything about it was warm and familiar and he melted against the man who'd opened his heart to a part of his life he hadn't even realized he was missing. He wasn't sure how long they stood there, wrapped in each other, but a sharp pain in his abdomen brought him back to reality. He broke away and stared down at the hilt of the knife sticking out of his gut.

His mouth fell open and a pained gasp tumbled out of him. He looked up at Jack, the obvious question on his lips, but Jack wasn't there anymore. Instead the man standing in front of him was clad in all black, hood drawn up to hide his face. Ryan tried to turn and run, but the stranger knocked him to the ground and pulled the blade out of his belly. Ryan wanted to see under the hood, tried to reach up and knock it away so he could look into the eyes of the man who was about to murder him, but the killer swatted his attempts away, closed both hands around the handle, raised the knife, and brought it back down, driving it into Ryan's heart. Ryan's blood spurt as the organ beat uselessly, pumping the final bits of his life into the air. He felt himself fading. But there was so much he hadn't done yet. So much he still wanted to say, and so many people he hadn't told he loved them in far too long. It was too late now. He tried to fight off the darkness, but it clawed at him, dragging him deeper and deeper until—

Ryan jerked awake. He was on the kitchen floor. Sunlight streamed in from the open curtains. He sat up and pressed a hand to his head. What time was it? Why had he drunk so much? Why did it feel like someone was sawing at his brain with a dull butter knife? He looked down to see a dark-gray stain in the crotch of his sweats. Had pissing himself pulled him out of the dream that was already slithering away from the reaches of his memory? He climbed to his feet, ignoring the warning throb in his skull and got the bleach and mop from the closet. As he cleaned up his mess, a sickening fact occurred to him. It was Friday. Jack's last day.

He'd spent the last two weeks begging for this day to come so he could be done with it already, but now that it was actually here, he wished he'd had more time. He didn't know if he'd be able to deal with it, especially not hungover. But he'd have to do what he'd have to do, because he was an adult. So even though it nearly killed him, he went upstairs, got in the shower, and got ready for what would surely be the worst day of his life.

CHAPTER TWELVE

How had Jack come to hate every suit he owned? Black. Blue. Dark gray. Black. Blue. Mahogany. Black. Blue. Black. Blue. Why the fuck did everything look like he was heading to a goddamn funeral? Even his ties were those muted, dreary colors. But maybe those were right for today. Nothing about the hours ahead of him called for anything happy.

He could just skip it, though, right? He didn't have to go. What were they going to do, fire him?

The thought comforted him even as he pulled one of those dark pieces of shit from his closet and started to slip it on. The oxygen left the room as he slid the pants on. Would death be easier than buttoning up his shirt? But what if it wasn't? Would he be stuck tying that same simple black tie for the rest of eternity? Or would shrugging into the jacket be his damnation? All because he couldn't be honest and open about his feelings in time. He deserved this.

Ryan was one of the best men he'd ever known. And Jack had hurt him. So why shouldn't he be miserable in return?

His phone rang as he picked it up to order a car to come get him. His mother. Again. She'd called a dozen times since his party, and he'd ignored every one of them. There couldn't be anything she was going to say that was going to make a damn thing better. Every moment of his life up to now had taught him that.

But once more, he let himself toy with the thought that maybe she had come around. And that was why she was calling. Maybe she wanted to tell him that she loved him no matter who he slept with and the hell with the rest of the family, she accepted him for who he was. Because that was what unconditional love was.

The thought was so powerful his vision shimmered and his hand trembled as he finally answered the call.

"Hello?" he said, hoping his voice was steadier than he felt.

"Good morning, Jackson." He knew that tone and already he could feel his heart cracking under the weight of it. He could just hang up now. What he was sure would be his last memory of the woman who'd given birth to him would be the one he'd created. But he couldn't bring himself to do it. For some reason he found himself rooted to the spot, hoping and praying that he was wrong.

"Good morning, Mother."

"I thought you'd like to know that your cousin had to go to the ER the other night. You broke his nose."

Usually, Jack would have been filled with savage pleasure that Cal had finally gotten what was coming to him after years of torment. But this wasn't the time for that.

"I see."

"He'll be pressing charges." Jack nodded, throat too dry to speak. She went on. "And we support him." There it was. Part of the reason she'd been trying to get in touch. But still, there had to be more. She could have told him that in a text. Or an email. No. She was only pressing the knife into his flesh now. The plunge was yet to come. She sighed. "I cannot believe you would embarrass us the way you did. We raised you better than that. But you don't seem to care about anything anymore. You only care about yourself. There's no other reason you could possibly have to . . ." Her voice faltered, and for one wild moment, Jack allowed himself to hope she felt remorse for what she was about to say.

"Ma . . ."

But this was a woman who'd never felt remorse about anything a day in her life. "You are no longer welcome in our home, Jackson. As far as we're concerned, your brother is our only son."

That was it. Though it had been exactly what he'd been expecting, Jack still had to grab the counter to steady himself. The air really had left the room. Fuck it to hell, when had he actually started to cry? Hot tears stung his face, and his heart shattered in his chest. It was one thing to imagine the words, but something else entirely to hear them.

This was the person who'd given him life. Now, here she was on the other end of the line telling him that she didn't love him anymore, all because of who he wanted to go to bed with.

She was still talking, he knew that, but he wasn't sure what she was saying. It didn't matter. He'd never see her again. Outside of court, that was. Because on top of everything else, he was being sued for defending himself against someone who had attacked him first. Wasn't that just the bee's fucking knees?

"You didn't have to tell anyone about your sickness," he finally heard her say. "We could have all gone on assuming the best, but no. You had to be selfish and let a room full of our closest friends know what kind of person you really are. And now when we walk past, they'll whisper. And they'll turn the other way when they see us on the street, because one was living right under our roof the entire time and we didn't even know." She paused and Jack prayed that she was done at last. But of course she wasn't. "The sin is in the scandal. Goodbye, Jackson."

The line went dead. For the last time.

He wanted to slit his wrists. To jump into the bay. To run out into traffic and let someone else end his suffering. But he couldn't do any of that. He wouldn't. Then they would win. His parents, and their friends, and everyone like them who'd ever thought someone like him shouldn't exist. That people like Ryan should be rounded up and taken out by a firing squad. And he wasn't about to let that happen. So he wiped his tears away and stood up tall. He was going to get through this. Even though now he was alone. He was going to be all right.

He requested his ride. And he went to work.

Jack had barely sat down at his desk and already he wanted to go back home. He'd known coming had been a bad idea, but what was the alternative? Being depressed at home? At least here he was more or less surrounded by people who wouldn't let him do anything stupid. And, probably most importantly, if he was at the office, he ran the chance of seeing Ryan one last time before his life went completely to shit.

The truth was that Jack didn't have another job lined up yet. When he walked out at the end of the day, he didn't know what was waiting for him. Yeah, quitting was stupid, but he couldn't just stay and continue making both of them miserable. The thought of simply breaking off their relationship and staying at the firm had crossed his mind more than once, but he didn't think he'd be able to do it. He knew Ryan too well. Cared about—*loved?*—him too much to put them both through that. No way he'd be able to stay away if both of them were still in the same place, so better to just make a clean break.

But it was hard doing that when he remembered how he'd been sitting right here when he'd sent that first text to Sheila. He'd spent most of that morning pacing, trying to decide whether reaching out to the drag queen was a good idea. The butterflies fluttering against the walls of his stomach had nearly stopped him, the thought of getting off with Sheila—*Ryan*—being a freak, one-time thing terrifying. But great ideas have a way of coming back and sticking with you. And his entire life had changed.

Now, with weeks between then and now, had it really been so great? If he'd never sent that text, he wouldn't be sitting here wishing he was anywhere else, with what was left of his heart threatening to explode. But he wouldn't change what had happened for the world. Ryan had opened Jack up to parts of himself that he'd been terrified to explore. And if that wasn't worth a little pain, what was?

He toyed with the idea of pulling out his phone and texting Ryan one last time, begging him to give him another chance, because what did he have to lose? But at that moment his secretary walked in.

"Mr. Kieza?"

"Yes."

"You have a visitor."

Jack resisted the urge to raise an eyebrow. He wasn't expecting anyone. All his clients had already been transferred to new attorneys and, though he was supposed to be boxing up the rest of his belongings, the movers weren't coming until later in the day. "Send them in, please."

His stomach roiled when Cal appeared in his doorway. A ferocious kind of happiness filled him at the sight of black and blue—there were those colors again—bruises painting his cousin's face, and the slight wince as he waited at the door, Jack's bisexuality an apparent repellant he couldn't yet get past.

Jack wasn't about to pretend he wasn't happy to see Cal had finally gotten his ass beat. But Jack shouldn't have been the one to do it. "What the fuck are you doing here?" he asked, not bothering to hide his snarl or the contempt in his voice.

Cal swallowed, another action that seemed to cause him physical pain. But there was something else there too. "Can I come in?"

"No. Whatever you have to say to me you can say right there. And then get the hell away from my office."

"I didn't do it," Cal said, chewing the corner of his mouth, gaze cast in the direction of the floor.

"Didn't do what?"

"What I said I did. The reason you beat the shit out of me. I didn't do it."

"The hell are you talking about?"

Cal stepped inside and closed the door behind him. Jack stood up, outrage curling his hands into fists. "You've done enough damage already. I'm warning you. Get the fuck out of here or so help me God—"

"Just sit down and shut up."

"What?" Jack's face was hot and rational thought was slowly edging itself out of his brain. The rage from last night started to return. "Do you want to—"

"I'm gay."

The words died in Jack's throat. He stood there stunned for a few seconds or what might have been a full hour before he said, "You're what?"

Cal looked at him straight on, bottom lip quivering. He took a deep breath. "You heard me. I said I'm gay." Jack fell back into his seat as his cousin stared at him. "I made it all up. Now can I please sit down?"

Jack wasn't sure if he believed it. But curiosity got the better of him, and he swept his arm out, inviting Cal into the seat across from him.

"I'm sorry," Cal said, suddenly refusing to meet Jack's eyes. "I shouldn't have hit you. I just . . . I couldn't let you say what you said and not do anything because everyone would have started asking questions. But I deserve what I got, and I'm sorry."

Jack asked the first question that came to mind. "How long have you known?"

Cal's Adam's apple bobbed, and he winced again. "High school. I, uh . . . I popped a woody in front of this guy after football practice one day, and he followed me into the locker room and blew me." He shook his head. "Never even tried to push him off. I'd been wanting it forever, and then he finally did it and . . . I begged him to fuck me right there and then let him smash every chance I got after that."

Jack didn't know where to start. So many questions he didn't really want the answers to, but he'd probably ask any way. "If it's been so long, why have you always been such a dick to me?"

For the first time, there seemed to be shame on his cousin's face. "I had an image. No one could know what I'd done, and the only way people wouldn't suspect anything was if I kept being an ass to you. At least, that's what I thought." He coughed and winced. "Everyone always thought you were. And the shit they said about you, man . . . I didn't want them talking about me that way."

"But you were fine joining in with them at my expense, huh?"

"Look, I know I'm a piece of shit. That's why I'm here. To apologize. For everything."

"And you think that's just supposed to make it all okay?"

"No. But I mean . . . it's a start right?"

"So what, we're supposed to suddenly be a family now? After all this time? I wasn't happy, but I was at least good with no one knowing. My mother disowned me this morning, all because you wanted to protect your fucking image!" He was on his feet now, shouting. He clenched his fists and slammed them on the desk. "My entire life is over," he said through gritted teeth. "Maybe I would have been a little braver if you would have just fucking talked to me. Knowing that I wasn't alone. That somebody had my fucking back. But now I've lost my family. I've lost the man that I love. I'm not going to have a job after today . . . I don't have anything."

There were tears in Jack's eyes again, but he didn't care. Let people judge all they wanted. "My entire life, I thought I'd been born wrong. Like there was something disgusting about me. But if you'd just . . ."

His voice broke and for a moment, he was at a loss for words. "If you'd just said something . . . I wouldn't have felt so fucking . . . alone."

Cal was next to him then, pulling him into a hug. "I'm sorry, man." There was agony in his voice, but whether it was physical or emotional, Jack didn't know. "I am so sorry."

He didn't know how long he stood there, crying into the shoulder of the man who'd made his childhood a living hell, but when he finally broke away, he collapsed into his chair. He didn't have any energy left. Not to stand. To talk. Hell, he didn't even know how he was breathing.

Cal closed his eyes briefly. "I know there's nothing I can say to make up for the things I've done, but I hope you can forgive me. That's what I really came here to say."

Jack scoffed. "You're pressing charges against me, and now you're asking me to forgive you?"

"I'm not. I only told them I was because they were pressing me, but I wouldn't do that. Not after everything."

"Small favors, I guess."

"Look, I'm gonna talk to your parents."

"Don't bother." Yeah, it hurt that the rest of his family wanted nothing to do with him, but in the long run, it was for the best. He didn't need people like that in his life.

"Well, know that you have me. I know that I haven't been, but whatever you need, whatever I can do . . . I'll be there."

"I'll believe that when I see it. But thanks."

Cal nodded. "I deserve that. But I mean it." He was silent for a moment, then, "I have a doctor's appointment, so I'm gonna get out of your hair, but you call me if you need me, yeah?"

"Sure."

"I mean it."

"Okay."

And then Cal was gone, and suddenly even less of Jack's life made sense than when he'd woken up that morning. But if Cal really meant what he'd said, then at least he wasn't by himself. Besides that, something else good had come of the visit. Courage bubbled in Jack, and he needed to take advantage of it before he lost his nerve. He had to talk to Ryan. Face-to-face.

And this time, he wasn't taking no for an answer.

CHAPTER THIRTEEN

Ryan massaged his temple as he reread the same line for the fourth time. He'd gone down the entire page, but when he'd gotten to the end, he'd realized none of the information had stuck and he'd started over. He tossed the paper to the side of his desk and pressed the heel of his hands against his eyes. He was completely useless today. The hangover was bad enough, but the grief of losing Dolly had made him totally stupid. He couldn't even get up and walk around, because he'd been hiding in his office since he'd gotten there so he wouldn't run into Jack, and now he was going stir-crazy.

His door banged open and when he looked up, Jack came into focus. Ryan ignored the tiny flip of his stomach and the flutter of his heart, and forced what he hoped was a cold expression onto his face. "Can I help you?"

"Don't do that to me." Jack sounded breathless, like he'd run up the hall. And why were his eyes all red?

"Excuse me?"

Jack closed the door behind him. "I've lost everything. My family. My job. My dignity. I'm not about to lose you too."

"This is not the place."

"Fuck that." Jack took a step forward. "You won't take my calls. You don't answer my texts. The only reason I haven't shown up at your door is I didn't think you'd answer it. So you tell me, Ryan. When is the time? Because when I walk out of this building today, you're never going to let me see you again."

"I don't want to see you."

"But I want to see you. I can't sleep. I can't eat. I can't . . . I can't function. I stood at my birthday party the other night hoping you were going to show. And you didn't." Another step. "I beat the shit out of my cousin because he was talking about bashing a drag queen and all I could think about was you. And it made me sick." Another. "I wanted to come to you after that and hug you . . . and kiss you . . . and protect you . . . but we're not us. I wanted to be there for you when I heard about Dolly, but I didn't think you'd answer. And I know that's my fault. And that I'm a dumbass. But I'm trying to be better. I'm trying to fix myself. I want to be a better man for you. But I can't do that without you. Without us. Because you help me be a better man. And I want to be there for you. With you. Whatever comes next."

Ryan's lip trembled. He wouldn't let himself cry. Wouldn't let the words he'd been wanting to hear for the last two weeks make him more vulnerable than he already was. So he pushed his emotions to the side. "You lost your chance."

Another step. "No. I haven't. And you know I haven't. Because if I told you that I wanted to fuck you right here and right now, you'd drop your pants and let me."

Ryan snarled. "I don't keep drag in my office."

"Do I look like I give a shit?"

Ryan's breath hitched. Now his stomach felt like it was curling in on itself and his cock was stiffening. "W-what?"

Another step. "Is that what it's going to take to prove to you how I feel about you? That I'm going to be better?" Jack closed the rest of the distance between them. God, he was so close Ryan could smell his cologne. He'd missed that delicious smell, and he had to swallow his inner slut before he really did drop to his knees and blow the man in front of him here and now. "I'm willing to risk any future I have working in this town to show you. Because I already told you how I feel. You thought the drag in the bedroom meant that I didn't want you for you. And now I'm ready to show you that I do. I didn't before, and I made you feel like you weren't good enough. But you always were. You were more than enough. And I'm ready to be the man for you."

"This is a place of business, Jack," he breathed.

"I don't care."

"But I do. One of us still has to come in here Monday morning." Ryan looked around. "Now will you please back up before someone sees you?"

Jack cast a glance toward the door. He truly looked like he didn't give a single fuck whether someone saw them or not. But then he went around the other side of the desk and sat down.

Ryan took a moment to compose himself, then asked, "Why should I believe you?"

"Come feel how hard my dick is and then tell me."

"Damn it, Jack! Not everything is about sex."

"No, but this is." Jack tilted his head and gave Ryan the full weight of his gaze. "Every other part of our relationship was great. You only broke up with me because I couldn't fuck you without the wig on."

"'Broke up'? You talk like we were actually dating."

"Oh cut the shit," Jack said, smiling playfully. "You were my boyfriend and you fucking know it. Every day I saw you. Went out of my way to spend time with you. Took you on dates. Cuddled you while we slept. I've never cuddled with anyone. So don't you stand there and tell me that we weren't dating."

Jack had a point, but Ryan wasn't about to tell him that. He wasn't going to give him the satisfaction. Not yet. "Okay, maybe we were."

"No. Not fucking maybe. You were my guy. And I was yours. And now I'm sitting here in your office, hard as a rock and ready to at least try to give you what you've been asking me for all along." Jack shook his head. "This stopped being about just sex for me a long time ago. But sex was the problem that broke us up, so I'm hoping that that's what's going to put us back together. Because I love you. And if you care about me as much as I care about you, these last two weeks have been hell for you, too. I'll do whatever I have to do to stop that and get you back. Or I'm at least going to try."

Ryan had heard every word Jack said, but one thing kept playing over and over again in his mind.

"I love you."

He wanted Jack to say it again, but he was afraid to ask in case he'd imagined it.

Jack seemed to read him. "You heard me. I love you. I love Ryan Andrew Swift, I love Sheila kick-you-in-the-balls Saltue . . . I love *you*. I know that I hurt you, but you mean too much to me to just let you walk away without giving it my all." He stood up, and now he was closing that space again. "So what do you say, baby boy? Are you gonna take me back?" He grabbed Ryan by the tie and pulled him into the corner of the room, out of view of the windows, so it was just the two of them, alone at last. "Or are you going to make me beg for it?"

Ryan stared at him for a moment. He closed the distance between them a fraction of an inch. He shouldn't want Jack so badly. Shouldn't need his touch. But he'd been strong for too long. So he gave in.

Jack brought their mouths together. Gently. Already, Ryan couldn't breathe as he melted into the kiss. God, how he'd missed this. Jack's hard body pressed against him, not to mention his dick flirting with Ryan's waist. He never wanted it to end—this was what his life had been missing, and now that it had come back, he'd be damned if he was going to let it go again.

Jack's hands fumbled with Ryan's belt, and Ryan tried to pull away, but Jack switched their positions and pushed him gently into the wall. He undid the belt, then the button, and shoved Ryan's pants down. Before Ryan could protest, Jack dropped to his knees and kissed the head of Ryan's cock. He licked from the base of the balls all the way up to the tip before turning him around and burying his face between Ryan's cheeks. Ryan let his eyes flutter closed as Jack tasted him, the sensation rolling over him with all the subtlety of an atom bomb. Jack hadn't done this nearly enough and, as Jack urged his tongue inside him, Ryan stifled a moan.

Jack alternated for a few moments between teasing and thrusting. Ryan was so hard he was surprised he hadn't shot his load already. This was the closest they'd come to sex out of drag, and Ryan wanted it to go on forever, which is why when Jack's tongue disappeared and his pants came back up, Ryan nearly screamed. But then they were face-to-face again, and Jack was kissing him, sharing his own flavor with him. When Jack pulled away this time, Ryan followed him, eyes still closed and lips poised for more.

"Nuh uh uh. That was just a preview of what's to come," Jack said. Ryan's eyes snapped open to find Jack grinning at him devilishly. "See you later, boss." He turned to leave, but stopped with his hand on the doorknob. He jerked his head in the direction of Ryan's hard-on. "And you better not do anything about that. I'll take care of it when I see you again." He winked and disappeared out into the hall.

Ryan let go of a breath and blinked rapidly, trying to clear his head. What the fuck had just happened? Ten minutes ago, he'd been sitting at his desk moping and hungover and now he had what felt like a piece of steel between his legs. If Jack came back right now and tried to fuck him, he damn sure wouldn't need any lube.

Straightening his tie, Ryan returned to his desk, scanning the outside of his office to make sure no one was looking his way, because hopefully that meant they didn't suspect what had happened in here.

He spent less than a minute toying with the idea of letting Jack back into his life before taking out his phone and practically punching in a text.

I changed my mind. I'm not accepting your resignation. Have your ass in my office at Close of Business.

He waited a minute for the reply and when it came he grinned.

I'm the one in control here. You don't tell me what to do.

Yeah? Well today the tables were turning.

I said what I said.

Another few seconds and then, *Yes, sir. Anything you say,* flashed across his screen. He dropped the phone back into his pocket and ran a hand through his hair, reclining in his chair. Now that his hormones were getting to a manageable range, he allowed himself the thought that this afternoon might not work out the way he wanted. What if Jack still couldn't get hard and wanted him to go break out a wig? How would he respond? Would he throw another fit and storm out, this time forever, or would it be the effort, ultimately, that swayed him to stay a little longer? Ryan didn't know.

But he couldn't wait to see how it turned out.

Jack didn't know what had come over him. When he'd walked into Ryan's office, his only plan had been to talk, to try to make Ryan see reason. Things had just ballooned out of control. But it had gotten him what he'd wanted, sort of, so he wasn't complaining. His dick was still straining against his underwear, begging to be free even as he imagined bending Ryan in all his manly glory over the desk. Hopefully he would be able to go through with it and his life could go back to normal. Whatever normal was.

He spent the rest of the day unpacking boxes, putting his office back together. A little premature, sure, but with the way the last few days had gone, he had no choice but to hope for the best. Not like things could get any worse.

So why, when the end of the day finally came, did he feel like he was going to be sick? He'd had sex with Ryan dozens of times since they'd met, this time couldn't be that much different. But as he walked out of his office and down the seemingly endless hallway toward Ryan's with the firm slowly emptying around him, the nausea in his guts swelled and it took serious effort not to dash off to the nearest bathroom.

A minute later, he knocked on Ryan's open door and the man inside looked up, all smiles for the first time in what felt like forever. Just like that, his nerves melted away and he wanted nothing more than to get this started. The sound of people still moving around behind him quashed that thought, though.

"You ready to get out of here?" Ryan asked, his voice husky. He couldn't have been trying to hide the lust in his eyes because they practically blazed with it.

Even if the two of them did try to leave, Jack wasn't sure they'd make it out of the building before Ryan jumped his bones. But Jack had other things in mind. "No way. I've got something better planned."

"Oh yeah? Like what?"

Jack stepped inside, didn't bother closing the door behind him. "I'm gonna fuck your lights out right here."

Ryan's face turned a deep shade of red. "The office is still full of people."

Fuck, that flustered look was cute. "Ask me if I care."

"Jack, really, we can't." His eyes darted around the room, seemingly searching for an escape, and Jack couldn't hold it anymore.

He let out a bark of laughter, doubling over with the relief of it. He hadn't laughed since he'd put in his resignation, and it felt great, like a boulder was rolling away from his chest. "You should see the look on your face."

"W-what?"

"Of course I'm going to wait for everyone to leave, dummy. I'm not about to risk the other partners finding out."

Ryan breathed a sigh and his expression softened. The corners of his mouth quirked into a grin, and Jack realized, once again, how hopelessly in love he was with the man sitting in front of him. It didn't seem right that they had met so late in his life, because they'd obviously been made for one another. And Jack planned to spend every day making Ryan feel as important and cherished as he was.

"But in the meantime," he said, taking the chair across the desk. "Did you already get another second chair for the Benning case?"

Ryan chuckled. "No. I've been putting it off. Guess I was hoping something like this would happen and you'd reconsider."

Jack shook his head. "There should have never been anything to reconsider. I was being selfish, and I'm sorry."

"I appreciate that. Hopefully you've got all of that out of your system. For Stephanie's sake. I've got a meeting with her Monday, and I'd like it if you came along so she can meet both of us face-to-face."

"Sure thing."

They spent the next hour or so discussing the details of the case, and Ryan explained the difference between drag queens and transgender people.

"Look, Sheila is a character," Ryan was saying, and Jack couldn't help but stare at the curve of his lips, the jut of his chin, the soft contours of his face. Even without the makeup, in the right lighting, he could pass for a gorgeous woman. "At the end of the day, I not only *can*, but I *want* to take her off. Drag gets exhausting, after a while. But for people like Stephanie Benning, it's not something they can slip in and out of. It's who they are. I put on my hair and my pretty dress and my makeup and suddenly . . . I'm Cleopatra, out for a night on the town, and people stare and they *Ooh* and *Ahh* and I love it, because I like being looked at. And they like to look." He shook his head. "But in most cases, trans people don't want to be gawked at. If they blend in with the crowd, more often than not, then they're safe." Ryan paused. He bit his top lip. "I already know this sounds shitty, but I can't think of a better way to say it, and it's pissing me off." He took a deep breath. "But it's the same way a lot of people in the community feel . . . If you don't stand out, don't make waves, people don't have a reason to fuck with you, you know? Not that we should have to cater to assholes. It's their problem, not ours, but it's still that constant fear."

Jack thought back to his fight with Cal the other night. "Doesn't mean that they won't." Then he remembered Cal's visit earlier and shook it away. That was a whole can of worms he wasn't prepared to deal with right now.

"True. But when someone at least *feels* safe, they're more content, usually. Which is what makes Stephanie's case so fucked up. She felt safe enough to let the people she worked with know who she really was and got fired for it."

"And now we're going to stick it to her boss."

"We're going to try to, anyway. I still don't know what judge we're going to get, and if it's one of the more conservative ones, we may be fucked." His gaze darted over Jack's shoulder, but Jack barely noticed. He was too wrapped up in what a shitty place this world was. Why couldn't people just be who they were without others feeling like they could put restrictions on them? He was so sick of hiding. Sick of everything that came with not wanting people to know the real him. Well he wasn't going to hide anymore. He'd stand up and be proud, regardless of what the consequences might be.

"No, we're going to give it to the bastard. If that's how he treats his people, then he doesn't deserve to be an employer." A plan had already started to roll around in Jack's brain, to be executed if they lost the case, but a foot trailing up and down his inner calf brought him back to the present.

Ryan stared at him with a slightly raised eyebrow and nodded toward the outer office. "Looks like everyone is gone, to me."

A grin split Jack's face and all thoughts besides those of the man in front of him were gone. He grabbed Ryan by the tie and pulled him into another kiss.

Jack couldn't believe he was doing this again, or how right it felt. He got out of the chair without breaking their connection, climbed on top of the desk, and got as close as he could. While their tongues battled, Jack worked at undoing Ryan's tie, then pushed the jacket off of his shoulders and unbuttoned his shirt. He ripped the shirt the rest of the way, smiling against Ryan's lips as the buttons hit the floor and scattered. Jack got off the desk and kissed his way down Ryan's body, sucking first one nipple, then the other between his teeth, rolling it and flicking at it until it was hard. He licked his way down Ryan's stomach, opening Ryan's belt and pants before going lower. Jack paused when Ryan's scent filled his nostrils. He'd never smelled anything more intoxicating, a mixture of some soft, feminine scent and an earthy aroma that almost had his mouth watering. But he'd never done this before. What if he was terrible at it?

"It's okay," Ryan said from above him.

Jack wasn't sure what, exactly, Ryan meant, but he took it as encouragement and gripped Ryan's cock before sucking the head between his lips. He traced it with his tongue, relishing the tiny hitch of breath from his boyfriend. He went an inch lower. Then another. Then another. And then fuck, he actually had a dick in his mouth and had no clue what to do. So he closed his eyes and pretended it was his own. If their positions had been reversed, what would he want done?

That did the trick.

He got Ryan's cock wet enough to stroke with both his hand and his tongue and used his other hand to fondle Ryan's balls. The body beneath his squirmed, Ryan muttering a string of curses Jack had never heard before, and it only spurred him on. Until Ryan pushed his head away.

"You gotta stop," he panted. "I'm about to blow."

"Good," Jack said, and if he was looking in a mirror, he was sure he'd see some sinister expression staring back at him. He dove back in and, a minute later, Ryan's hand reappeared. This time, Ryan shoved Jack's head down as his hips bucked forward and his cock slipped farther down Jack's throat.

Fuck. It hadn't been that deep before. Jack's eyes watered and he gagged, feeling Ryan's stomach rumble as he groaned. He gagged again, but held it back because he could feel Ryan's cock pulsing between his lips. A mingle of bitter and sweet danced on his taste buds and the back of his mouth was suddenly full. He knew it wasn't just saliva, so he pushed what he could to the back of his throat, took a breath through his nostrils, and swallowed. Ryan's body seized, jerked, and went limp. Jack used one hand to wipe away his tears while squeezing Ryan's dick between the thumb and forefinger of the other, dragging them up and drawing out every drop. Ryan released a slow, shaky breath as Jack kissed his way back up his body, then paused and practically breathed against his neck, "You wanna taste?"

"Fuck yeah," Ryan growled before crushing their mouths together. He seemed to be searching for traces of himself, and it turned Jack on more than ever before. He was still hard, and fuck, he wanted to get it done before his body betrayed him. But he couldn't. Not yet. There was still prep work to be done, and that taste of Ryan's ass he'd gotten earlier had only been a tease. He wanted more.

"Get up and bend over."

Ryan did as he was told. Jack knelt behind him, parted his ass cheeks and dove in. Ryan's moans went up an octave as Jack probed him, tracing his taint before sticking his tongue in and curling it back as though trying to beckon another orgasm. Jack feasted, doing things with his tongue he hadn't even known were possible. The higher Ryan's voice went, the more Jack gave, until he couldn't take it anymore. He hadn't been with anyone else, and he prayed Ryan hadn't either as he stood up. "Tell me you've got a condom."

"Do we need one? Really?" Ryan asked.

Thank God. "Fuck no." The sight of Ryan beneath him was the most beautiful thing he'd ever seen. Ryan's head hung off the desk with his arms stretched out to either end, clutching the edges as though his life depended on it.

"Don't you fucking move," Jack said, undoing his zipper and letting his cock spring free, still mercifully hard. He spat in his hand stroked himself, staring at Ryan's bubble butt. Fuck, it looked almost as amazing as it had tasted. So why had Jack gotten less firm? Maybe he hadn't been as hard as he'd thought.

No. Please, God, no. But he was definitely getting smaller, and one glance told him that Ryan had loosened his grip on the desk. Jack couldn't let him know anything was wrong, so he sank to his knees again and continued lapping at the man beneath him. This couldn't be happening. He'd been solid the entire fucking time, so why when it came time to actually do the damn thing had his body turned on him? What kind of self-sabotaging shit was that?

He gave his mouth a break and circled a finger around Ryan's hole before letting it sink in to the second knuckle. He added a second finger and used them, scissoring and working them in and out, curling them until they found Ryan's prostate.

"Please," Ryan whimpered. "I need you."

Jack was definitely hard again, but he didn't trust himself to stay that way. He replaced his fingers with his tongue and started to stroke himself again. His cock had dried, but it didn't matter because if he couldn't stay hard once he stood up, he wouldn't be able to get it in, lubricated or not. He said one more prayer, got to his feet, did his best to spit downright onto the head of his cock, and pressed his way inside.

Shit, Ryan was even tighter than he remembered. How long had it been since he'd been inside him? And it definitely felt better without a condom. Ryan's walls were slick and silky, and they caressed him as Ryan squeezed around him.

Jack was still hard. There didn't seem to be any sign of waning, and damn it, that was all he needed. He grabbed Ryan's hip with one hand and his shoulder with the other, and then he was *fucking* him. Harder than he'd ever done it before. But he knew Ryan was loving every inch of it, because he was pressing back, bouncing and dancing like he'd never be fucked again. It was happening. Jack was inside a man. All man. No wig. No makeup. No illusion at all, and it was the most incredible thing he'd ever felt, because he'd never felt so close to Ryan as he did now.

"Fuck . . . me . . . fuck . . . me . . . fuck . . . me . . ." Ryan sang, and Jack obliged. He'd keep this going for as long as he could, but that wouldn't be long—his orgasm was already starting to build at the base of his balls. Jack didn't dare try to stave it off because, with his luck, he'd lose his hard-on completely and this would all be for nothing. One look at the way Ryan's ass swallowed him, clapping around his dick was all it took. Jack grunted, and before he could say anything, he blew his load, coating the inside of Ryan with everything he had to offer.

But the high was short-lived. Through the haze, he noticed a shadow at the other end of the hall, and the door was still open, so they had no cover. Jack lifted Ryan, pulled him back and to the floor.

"What the fuck—" Ryan started before Jack clapped a hand over his mouth.

"Someone's coming," he hissed.

Jack had expected panic, a frantic effort to pull clothes back on. Something. But instead he got, "But I'm not done yet." Ryan cast a glance over his shoulder. "Lean back." Stunned, Jack did as he was told, which told him that they were completely under the cover of the desk. Or, at least, he was.

And it was then that he noticed that he was still inside Ryan. And still hard as a fucking rock, because Ryan started bouncing on his cock again. Jack bit his lower lip and let his head hit the wood behind him. He couldn't believe what was happening, but why fight it? The risk of getting caught was thrilling. He hadn't felt anything like it since that night in the alley, and he was all for it. The footsteps were getting closer, and Ryan's hand was working furiously between his own legs.

The sound of rolling wheels echoed down the hallway. It was the custodian emptying trash cans, which gave them a minute, maybe two, to finish. Jack was already on the verge of another climax, but he did his best to hold it back, because he wanted to come with Ryan this time. So he let himself feel and enjoy what was happening to him, but he imagined the sullen look on the janitor's face as he went floor to floor, cleaning up after people who likely had no respect for him. And the sounds grew closer still. Ryan was clenching him harder, and Jack looked down to see thick, white ropes on his dick, getting Ryan's ass wetter and pushing them both closer to the edge of oblivion.

"I'm about to come," Ryan breathed at last.

"Thank God." Jack held Ryan's hips in place and bucked his hips up, trying to hit one of Ryan's spots. It must have worked, because Ryan gave a strangled cry and his body seized again. Jack let go and they came together. Stars exploded in front of his eyes. After a moment Jack became aware that the sounds outside the office had stopped. He put a hand on Ryan's back to still him and listened. Finally, he heard a small groan.

"Great. More sex stains. I don't get paid enough for this."

And then the wheels were retreating. Jack thought Ryan would be horrified, but instead he collapsed into a fit of laughter, sliding off Jack's cock and rolling onto his back. Jack couldn't help it. He laughed too.

"Get over here and kiss me."

Jack did as he was told.

"I love you too," Ryan said.

They were the most beautiful words Jack had ever heard.

CHAPTER FOURTEEN

Four hours. Jack had been back in Ryan's life *officially* for four hours, and Ryan had never been happier. Already, he was dreaming up new numbers for Sheila and, though he wouldn't admit it to Jack, he might have been planning a holiday vacation somewhere exotic.

Maybe a little premature, sure, but the smell of dinner wafting out from the kitchen was scrambling his brains and making him believe that happily ever after might not only be possible, but finally within his reach.

He turned on the television, and his elation vanished the second he saw the flashing Breaking News banner across the bottom of the screen.

No. Not again.

He didn't want to turn up the volume. Didn't want to know if another one of his friends was lying dead in the morgue, but his body moved as though on autopilot.

"Police are now instituting a mandatory curfew for all citizens until the culprit is apprehended. Once again for those just tuning in: the body of another drag performer has been found, this time identified as simply Angel."

He hadn't known Angel well—she was new to the club—but that didn't make her death sting any less. Someone was murdering his friends, and there weren't a lot of them left. He could be next. Wouldn't that be something? Now that his life had finally started falling into place, it would be time for a psycho to come knock him off like some dummy in a scary movie.

"What's wrong?" Jack asked from a million miles away.

"They found another body," Ryan heard himself say, and was horrified by the lack of emotion in his voice.

Second body.

Two days.

Whoever was behind the killings was getting bolder.

"You don't need to be watching this," Jack said, gently slipping the remote from his hand and turning off the TV.

"What does it matter? I'm going to die, anyway." The edges of Ryan's vision shimmered and despair clawed at his insides. "Whether I see what's happening or not. He's coming for me. He's coming for all of us. And he's not going to stop until we're all dead. He's going to kill me."

"No," Jack said, taking Ryan's face in his hands and forcing him to meet his gaze. "I will never let that happen."

Ryan scoffed. "How are you going to stop it?"

"Look, no one knows you're a drag queen. And Neon Trees isn't doing any more shows until he's caught, right? There is nothing that's putting you in danger until this is all over."

"I can't just not perform." The thought of not getting done up and giving the people what they wanted—what he *needed*—would kill him faster than some crazy with a knife ever could. Performing was his outlet. It was as essential to his life as breathing. He needed the comfort it brought him, or the stress might take him out. Tears prickled the edges of his eyes.

"Yes, the fuck you can. This is your life we're talking about. I just got you back. I'm not about to lose you again."

Ryan had never seen that fire in Jack's eyes before. It was endearing, if not a little terrifying. An even scarier possibility was Jack asking him to promise that he wouldn't take the stage again until they knew they were in the clear. He couldn't honestly agree to that, because what if they were never in the clear? Thankfully, Jack never did. Instead, he pulled Ryan into his arms and held him while Ryan cried. What else could either of them do here?

Ryan's dream floated back to him. What if the killer really knew where he lived? Had found out his secret, somehow? Even though he knew it wasn't possible, Ryan let the thought light a fire inside him. He was in danger, there was no doubt about that, but he couldn't live his life in fear. What he could do was stand up. Lead the charge and show this maniac that they weren't afraid of him. That he was just a terrorist and he wasn't about to dim their sparkle.

By the time Ryan and Jack sat down to dinner, Ryan had an entire event plan tumbling around in his brain. But he had to find girls who'd be willing to do it. And someone who would host them.

"You're planning something stupid, aren't you?" Jack asked through a mouthful of alfredo.

"I am," Ryan said resolutely. "Are you going to try to stop me?"

Jack put down his fork and surveyed him. "Even if I do, it's not going to do any good. I just want you to promise me I'm not going to have to be called in to identify you."

"Scout's honor."

There was no way Ryan could stick to that promise, and he was sure Jack knew that too. But it meant the world that Jack was willing to let him do this without putting up a fight. He'd undoubtedly be hovering in the wings the entire time, anyway.

That was fine, though. Added protection.

Once they were done with dinner, Ryan excused himself while Jack did the dishes. The walk upstairs seemed to stretch on forever. Suddenly paranoid, his eyes darted to every shadow. He marked every possible hiding place. He didn't want to believe he'd be attacked in his own home, but he had to face it, if the killer did decide to come here, the place was a fucking death trap. He steeled himself and swallowed his fear once again. The faces of all the fallen girls flashed through his mind as he went into his office. He was doing this for them.

Valentine.

Taylor.

Dolly.

Angel.

Hell, even Simon, if the bastard had gotten to him too.

Ryan sat down at his desk and pushed a sketch of one of Sheila's new outfits to the side. He admired it for a second, falling in love with it all over again. It would be perfect for what he was planning. Now, not only was he letting Sheila save his life, he hoped by the time they were done, other queens would have the courage to not live in fear of what might happen when they stepped out of the house. Smiling, he tucked the idea of the dress into a corner of his mind.

There would be time for that, but first, he had calls to make.

"You know you don't have to do this, right?" Ryan asked. Jack appreciated him being here. He was sure part of Ryan's mind was back home, still planning the event he'd dreamed up, but he'd taken time away from that to be by Jack's side.

Jack stood staring at the door to the restaurant, his heart beating an entire symphony against his rib cage. This was a terrible idea and he knew it, but there was a part of him that needed to see them one last time, have them tell him to his face that he was dead to them. Then, hopefully, he'd be able to move on.

"Yes. I do."

He hadn't wanted Ryan to come. He didn't want to give his family any more reason to be hostile than they already had. But Ryan had insisted. *I'm not about to let you throw yourselves to the lions and not be there by your side,"* he'd said when Jack had approached him with the idea. *"You're not in this alone anymore."*

"I'm gonna go in," Jack said now, trying to keep the fear whispering in his ear from forcing him to tuck his tail and run.

Ryan placed a reassuring hand on his back. "You take as long as you need. I'm right here."

After a few more minutes, Jack straightened his tie, nodded to Ryan, and the two of them went inside.

The restaurant was busier than he'd expected. Every table was full and waitstaff bustled from one end to the other.

"Can I help you?" the man at the host stand asked. He wore the restaurant's blue and black—there were those colors *again*—uniform and his blond hair up in a man-bun. His thick beard practically screamed hipster, and his air gave off the impression that he was over everything about this place.

Jack scanned the room, looking everywhere except at the man in front of him. He still had time to call it off. They never even had to know he was here. Even though he once again had started to allow himself the foolish thought that things would work out the way he wanted them to. That he'd leave here tonight with his family intact once again. That wouldn't be the case. And for the life of him, he couldn't figure out why he felt like he needed to put himself through it. Fuck closure. Sanity was better.

Even worse than whatever they'd throw at him, Ryan would see what kind of people they really were. What kind of stock he came from. That possibility terrified him more than anything else.

Ryan's hand on his shoulder brought Jack back to reality. He looked in Ryan's direction, his mind a little hazy. "What?"

Ryan nodded gently at the host, who had an impatient eyebrow raised.

"Oh. Sorry. Jack Kieza. There should be a reservation under my name."

The man consulted his list, tapping his pen against the stand. "Right this way," he said, never looking back up at them. They followed him, Jack mapping potential escape routes.

The atmosphere calmed him a little. The *clink* of silverware hitting china, the soft lighting, the classical musical floating down at them from the speakers. Jack had chosen this place because he'd hoped it would put his parents at ease. It would certainly stop him from making the same kind of scene he'd made at his birthday party. But anxiety still pressed in on him, not quite suffocating anymore, but if he'd had any Xanax, he certainly would have popped a pill or two. Maybe even three. Just for good measure.

It felt like they'd been walking forever, and he allowed himself the hope that maybe his family had decided not to show. Or that they'd gotten tired of waiting and left. As soon as the thought formed in his mind it was dashed. His mother came into view, spooning soup into her mouth. His father was saying something, and his sister and brother were deep in conversation. Even Cal and his mother were there. He'd only invited his immediate family, but of course they'd invited others along too. Just fucking perfect. But this would be Cal's chance to prove what he'd said in his office.

Jack locked eyes with his mother, and she nudged his father, who in turn alerted the others, and then they were all looking at him. Like he was some kind of leper or something. He wanted to shrink into himself. Wanted to take off and not stop running until the world made sense again. But there was Ryan's hand again, this time closing around his own. Such a small gesture, but he drew strength from it, because God knew he'd need it to get through this dinner. His sister's gaze dropped to that connection and she snarled. She mouthed something that looked suspiciously like *Fucking faggots*, before trying to flag down their waiter. Anger bubbled in his stomach at that, but he did his best to soothe it. This wasn't the place.

"Hey, everybody," he said, first pulling out Ryan's chair and then his own. The waiter appeared and his sister asked for another glass of wine. Filled to the top. And if he could just bring the whole bottle, it would be great.

Their collective gaze had shifted to Ryan, and Jack felt the instant need to protect. He wouldn't let them turn their anger on Ryan, because Ryan hadn't done anything but love him. Something the rest of the people at this table seemed suddenly incapable of doing. "This is Ryan," he said. He swallowed, throat dryer than the desert. He scanned the table for an untouched glass of water, didn't find one, took a deep breath, and dove in. "My boyfriend."

His father's face twisted into a mask of rage. "Is this why you brought us here?" he hissed, the effort to keep from shouting apparently great. He'd turned a deep shade of red and his nostrils flared. "To flaunt your unnatural shit in our faces?"

"No," Jack said, trying to sound stronger than he felt. "I asked you all here because this has gone on for too long. I've been hiding for too long and I'm just . . . I'm tired." He shook his head, fought back the building tears. He chanced a glance at Cal, whose look of disgust mirrored everyone else's except Aunt Sasha's. Her face was blank as she peered at him intently, fingers steepled under her chin.

"I know that none of you are probably going to ever want to see me again after tonight, but I have to try. Because . . . for the first time in a really long time . . . I'm happy. I feel like I'm free, and I have this man sitting next to me to thank for it." He put a hand over Ryan's.

His mother had remembered the pearls tonight—because now she clutched them. She and his father seemed to be in a competition to see who could flare their nostrils the most. Jack had thought his father might have attacked, or stormed out by now. Maybe the fact that he hadn't meant there was hope. Jack pressed on.

"I know you're worried about how everyone else is going to look at you if they find out, but I'm asking you . . . begging you . . . don't turn your back on me." He swallowed. Now the tears were prickling the edges of his eyes. He wouldn't be able to hold them back much longer. "This is the best me I can be. Right here in front of you. And I don't want to hide from it anymore. I want to be who I am. And I want to love who I love. And all I want you to do is support me because . . . you're my family."

Now the tears were falling, leaving hot, wet trails down his face. No one said a word, so he went on.

"I know you don't understand it. I know you hate it. Hell, you might even hate me right now, but I love all of you. More than you know." He faltered. What would Sheila do in this situation? She'd be on stage in some gown, single spotlight trained on her, belting all of this out as a power ballad, probably. Ryan put his other hand on top of his and squeezed. Jack sniffled.

"I just need you to not give up on me. Not because of this. I know that this is a blow to all of you. It probably hurts. And God knows you guys have hurt me. But I can look past it. Because I still want to be a part of your lives. I want you to be a part of mine. Because you mean more to me than some dumb shit in the past." His bottom lip trembled as he wiped away his tears. "I hope I mean more to you too." He turned his attention to Cal, whose lips were parted slightly. His face had softened and he no longer looked like he wanted to jump across the table and bash Jack's face in. "I'm sorry for what I did to you. I should have kept my temper, and I didn't."

"But that's my fault," Ryan said. Everyone's gaze turned back to him. Everyone's but Jack's mother's. She took her napkin from her lap and placed it over her soup bowl as though she could no longer bear the sight of it.

"You don't have to do this," Jack said, giving Ryan his most pleading eyes.

"Of course I do," Ryan said, nodding. "Why should you be the only one exposing yourself right now?" He turned back to the people sitting across from them. God, they felt like a jury. Jack knew that the chance of this particular verdict coming back in their favor was slim to none, but he still wished they would at least say *something*. "Jack told me what happened and I feel bad about it because the only reason he attacked you is because . . . I am a drag queen."

Jack wished he hadn't said that, because it wasn't true, but contradicting Ryan here would likely do more harm than good.

Ryan undid the top couple of buttons of his shirt, and Jack could see a flash of blue sequins sparkling there.

Jack's brother looked like he was going to be sick, his father made a fist around the bit of tablecloth he was holding, and his mother got up.

"I'm not going to sit here and listen to this anymore. Your father is right. The only reason you called us here was so you could rub this in our faces, and shame on you. You think that *this*," she gestured at Ryan, "is best for you. That he brings out the best in you?" She shook her head. There were tears shining in her eyes as well. "I would rather be dead than listening to this right now. And you may as well have just stuck a knife in my gut because that's what it feels like. Like you've stabbed me and spat in my face, after all I've done for you. I just don't know where I went wrong."

"You're doing it right now," Aunt Sasha said.

"Excuse me?"

"Your *son* is sitting in front of you. Risking everything. Begging you to accept him even though he knows as well as I do that you're a bunch of jackals." Now they were looking at her. Jack's mouth opened. He didn't think he'd ever heard his aunt talk like that, let alone to her sister. "God knows why he loves you all the way he does, because you've done nothing but make his life miserable and anybody with eyes can see it, but he does. And you're all just going to turn your backs on him?"

"Stay out of this, Sasha!" his mother shrieked. Jack had obviously been wrong about them not making a scene because they were in a fancy restaurant. "You don't know what this is like! What we're going through right now."

"Oh, I don't? You think you're the only one with a queer for a son?"

Jack made a mental note to educate his aunt on language later.

Cal blinked. He'd been looking down at the table for the last few minutes, but now his eyes were on his mother. "Ma . . . you knew?"

"Oh please," she said, putting a hand on his shoulder. "I've known since you were fifteen. You weren't good at clearing the computer history and then I caught that boy with his dick up you—"

"That's enough!" Jack's father said, jumping to his feet with such force that the table rattled. "It's bad enough that we have to listen to one of them," he jerked his head in Jack's direction, "but now you're telling us that another one has been under our noses the entire time?"

"You'd best watch what you say," Aunt Sasha said, giving her brother-in-law a warning stare. "Your son may not do anything, but if you dare say a word against my son the way you've been talking about your own, there's going to be a big problem here."

"I don't have to listen to this," he said.

"Then don't. Leave. Run away like you always do. Turn your back on this man that you created. Who was brave enough to face you all down knowing full well that you'd leave him out in the cold because you're all a bunch of heartless cowards."

That did it. "Well I guess you're dead to me too," his mother said. She snatched her coat from the back of the chair and stormed off toward the door. Her husband and daughter followed, but Jack's brother stayed behind, leveled Ryan with a stare.

"You're going to pay for this," he said with a snarl. "You and all the other little trannys like you." His snarl curled into a demented smile. "But you already know that, don't you?" He winked, grabbed a breadstick, and followed the rest of his family toward the door.

Jack put an arm around Ryan, who was visibly shaken. He didn't want to believe what he'd just heard.

"I'm sorry the two of you had to go through that," Aunt Sasha said. Jack turned in her direction. "I've always loved you and I always will," she said. "I accept you just the way you are." She stroked her own son's face gently. "And I'm guessing now that his secret is out, your cousin will too."

Jack got up and embraced first his aunt, then Cal. He turned back to Ryan, who was paler than he'd ever seen him. A thin sheen of sweat stood on his forehead. "I . . . I can't be here," he said. God, he was trembling.

"Yeah," Jack said. "I'm going to get him out of here," he said to the only two family members he had left. "Thank you. I'll call you. I promise."

"You're not going anywhere by yourself," Cal said. "I don't trust them. I'll drive you."

"Are you sure?"

"Of course. I told you, I'm here for you."

Jack looked from Ryan to his aunt, feeling slightly helpless. He was at war with himself. Logic told him there was no proof his brother was a killer. That threat kept echoing in his mind, though.

"I'll pay the bill, don't worry about it. Just get out of here," she said.

He nodded and then helped Ryan out of his chair.

Cal escorted them outside, sparing an extended glance at the hipster host on their way out the door. It was odd, but Jack brushed it away. The others had gone already, but that didn't mean that he and Ryan were safe. What if his brother really was the killer? He could be waiting in the shadows for them and they would never know. They'd never see him coming. Just like the other queens hadn't.

The lights on Cal's pickup flashed as the doors unlocked, and Jack climbed into the backseat with Ryan. "You don't mind, do you?"

"Of course not."

Jack wondered if Ryan was rethinking his event. It was only two days away now, but he didn't want to ask in front of Cal. His boyfriend was vulnerable already without him pressing anything with someone else around. Jack gave his cousin his address—he wasn't about to tell anyone where Ryan lived, not until he was sure it was safe—and settled back with Ryan nestled against his shoulder.

The night had gone almost exactly the way he'd thought it would, though he hadn't counted on Aunt Sasha coming to his rescue. It was nice knowing that he did still have people on his side. He pulled Ryan a little closer to him, tried to project a calm that he didn't feel. Ryan stopped shaking eventually and his breathing grew deep. A moment later, his light snores filled the back of the truck.

"You really do love him, huh?" Cal asked. Jack saw him peering at them through the rearview.

"I really do. He's helped me more than I can ever say. I don't know where I'd be without him."

Cal chuckled. "Maybe one day I'll be able to find someone like that too." He looked, almost mournfully, back at the road.

Something had happened to his cousin. Something Jack had never noticed because he'd always thought he hated him. But this wasn't the time to ask.

Jack was wrecked. He hadn't felt so emotionally drained since the *last* time he'd talked to his mother, and he needed to recover, so they rode in silence for the rest of the journey. When they pulled up to his place, he helped Ryan out and went back to the window. "I'll call you," he told Cal. "I don't even know how to thank you for all of this."

"Just don't let anybody force you back into the closet, yeah? This is a good look on you."

Now it was Jack's turn to chuckle. "Promise." He nodded another thanks and took Ryan up to his apartment. Once they were inside, they plopped down on the couch, not bothering to take off their nice clothes. Jack reached for the remote, but Ryan stopped him.

"Please don't do that." A tear fell that Jack wiped away. "Someone else might be dead and, if they are, I don't want to know. Not tonight."

Jack understood, so they sat there, silence blossoming around them until Ryan fell asleep once again. Jack snuck away long enough to change out of his suit and to grab a blanket. He sat back down as gently as he could—Ryan was going through enough and Jack didn't want to wake him. He'd been all but threatened tonight and, in less than forty-eight hours, he and twelve other entertainers were putting their lives on the line again. All to show some madman that he wouldn't terrify them into silence. That the night was theirs. And they were taking it back.

Jack glanced at the door to make sure it was locked, and then followed Ryan off to sleep.

CHAPTER FIFTEEN

This club was smaller than the normal one. And I hated the name: The Reputation Room. But it's where the bitches had decided to make their stand; they'd wanted me here, so here I was. I crumpled the flyer in my pocket; it had told me everything I needed to know.

I could respect bravery; it was an admirable trait in anyone. The first one had been brave, and that's what had inspired me to slash *his* throat from ear to ear. And then the second one . . . The bitch just wouldn't shut up; and the blood spurting in my face from the severed artery had been so satisfying. There hadn't even been a hint of fear until he'd realized what was about to happen. The only reason I hadn't dropped my pants and stroked one out right then had been because it would have left DNA.

But this . . . this spectacle wasn't about bravery. It was about defiance. And I hated being defied. I'd slaughter every single one of them on stage tonight if I could.

There were more people in the club than I'd thought there would be. At first, I'd thought it was because I hadn't inspired enough fear in the people, but then I realized, they must have figured that since they weren't strutting around all done up like sluts, they were safe. And maybe they were right.

I didn't want the men who actually knew they were men. I only wanted the bitches. And a dozen of them were here tonight, under one roof, taunting me, practically begging to be the next headline. And they would be. I wished there was a way I could have taken all of them out tonight. But it would have had to be one by one.

Movement out of the corner of my eye caught my attention. Another police officer. Fourth one I'd seen tonight. I gritted my teeth.

Their increased presence tonight was troubling, but it wasn't anything I couldn't handle.

I ordered a drink and watched as the bitches paraded through their acts one by one, until there was only one left. One I'd seen before.

The man swept onto the stage, more sissy in his walk than a gay on the runway for the first time. Gone was that gown he'd performed in last time; it had been replaced by a pair of thigh-high red boots, a shimmering red dress that stopped maybe an inch before the shoes began, and a long blonde wig. "How the hell is everyone doing tonight?" he shouted into the mic, and the crowd erupted into applause. He waited until they finished, flipping that fake hair over his shoulder like he actually thought he was a real woman. A smile spread across his face. "Ladies . . . gentlemen . . . and everyone somewhere in the middle or still trying to figure it out . . ." He tilted his head and let out a small laugh. "I want to thank you so much for coming out tonight. My name is Sheila Saltue and I organized this event." Another thunderous roar from the audience. "As I'm sure you've all heard, there's someone out there attacking us. Murdering us. Hiding in the shadows like a coward, and trying to scare us away from doing what we love."

Oh I'm not hiding anywhere, sweetheart. I'm right here. Right under your nose. Not my fault you're too self-absorbed to see me.

"And this is my way of telling him: FUCK YOU!" Now there was stomping with the clapping, a chorus that made me even more sorry I hadn't brought along something deadlier than my usual knife. "We won't be silenced. We won't live in fear. We're going to keep doing this, because this is what we do." A pause. "I hope he's watching right now. Because I'm about to give him something to see. Are you all ready to be entertained one more time?" The man on stage shouted this last part, and their applause was drowned out by the music blaring to life over the speakers.

I didn't even know what the bitch was singing about this time. Anger coursed through every part of me; I could almost hear the rush of blood in my ears. I didn't like being mocked, and just like that, I didn't give a shit about the rest of them, even as they filed on stage to join their *fearless leader* for what I could only assume was the final number. I made a note of every one of their faces and filed it away.

They were safe, because tonight my sights were only set on one: that bitch in the middle. That mouthy little faggot was going to pay for every single word he'd just said.

With his life.

Ryan couldn't remember an evening going more perfectly. They'd had to go to the next county over to find a club willing to host the event, but it had all been worth it. Even now as he slid off his tights and untucked—the only de-dragging he'd be doing tonight—he was still riding high. A couple of the other girls clapped him on the shoulder as they passed.

"I have never been more proud of you," a voice came from behind him. He spun around, instinctively shoving the dress back down to cover himself.

"Oh please," Justine said. "I've probably touched that thing just as much as you have. Someone didn't like to tuck in the beginning, remember?"

This was a cherry, if he'd ever seen one. Shame cast aside, he threw his arms around his drag mother and squeezed. He couldn't put into words how happy he was to see her, so he just held her, trying to absorb her strength for once the adrenaline wore off. Finally, he let go and backed away.

"Were you here the entire time?" He wanted to say that those weren't tears prickling the corners of his eyes, but it would have been a bald-headed lie.

"Where else would I have been? Queens all over the place have been talking about this nonstop for the last two weeks."

Ryan's insides swelled with pride. "Why didn't you say something?"

"Because I wanted to see you in action. Couldn't do that if you knew I was watching, could I?"

A shiver of unease ran down Ryan's spine. God, he wished Justine had worded that a little differently. He tried to shake it off as he pulled one of his boots back on. "I, um, I didn't think we'd have the turnout we did. But it looks like people really do support us. Either that, or they just wanted to get out and have a good time. But either way, I'm good. I made a killing today and everybody had fun, so that's all that matters."

"Of course it's all that matters. But you know how it goes, give people a reason to get shit-faced, and you'll have them beating down your door. Shit, give someone enough of a reason to do anything and they'll be there. It's just human nature."

Something was off about Justine. Ryan couldn't put his finger on exactly what it was, but for starters, he wasn't the biggest fan of the way she was looking at him. Like she was sizing him up or something. And now that he was *really* seeing her, he noticed more. She wasn't nearly as put together as usual. She'd hardly put on any makeup— lipstick and a little mascara *maybe*—her wig was off-center with the lace standing out in stark contrast with her dark skin. Even her clothes were rumpled, like she'd just pulled them out of a bag, or something. The Justine he knew would *never* be seen in public like that. Her cardinal rule had always been to never step out of your house unless you looked like you were about to meet the most important person in the world. The one you wanted to impress the most. Because at the end of the day, this was female *illusion*.

So where was hers?

He nearly tore the zipper of his boot he was moving so fast, because suddenly, he didn't want to be here anymore. Something was very wrong. It might have been his anxiety, kicking into overdrive because he hadn't taken his meds before he'd come here, but he'd never know for sure until he was out of this room and could think more clearly.

An idea started to form and he swatted it away, because he damn sure wasn't about to go there.

That shiver of unease had blossomed into full-blown panic, and as Ryan collected his things from around the dressing room, trying to maintain a calm air. He found his gaze kept falling to Justine's purse. It was definitely large enough to hold a knife. Hell, if she wanted to be crafty, she could have hid the damn thing in her dress. Clubs around the city checked the customers for weapons, but no one ever bothered to check the queens. They were only there to entertain. Why would one of them ever want to hurt anyone?

A piece of a puzzle Ryan hadn't even realized he'd been putting together fell, unwanted, into place as his own words floated back to him. Why would the killer need to hide in the shadows when it was so much easier to hide in plain sight? When you'd put in your time and paid your dues and everyone *trusted* you. Drag queens, as a general rule, were not a very gullible bunch; too many people disliked them, even in the gay community, so they had to be on their toes at all times. So who better to pick them off then someone who was already a member of the inner circle?

Ryan didn't want to believe it. He wanted it to be crazy. He wanted his brain to come up with literally any other scenario, but it made too much sense. Valentine had been the first victim. Only a few days after she and Justine had had another of their arguments.

"Are you all right?" Justine asked, and Ryan realized then that neither of them had said a word in at least two full minutes.

"Yeah, I'm fine," he said, hoping his voice didn't betray how definitely not fine he was. "I just need to get home. My boyfriend is waiting for me and he made dinner to celebrate tonight."

"Oh?" Justine cocked her head a little to the side. "Why didn't he come tonight? Doesn't he know about you?"

"Of course he does. He just wasn't feeling well." That wasn't true. Jack had been demanding to come since Ryan had told him about his idea. It was literally five minutes before he'd walked out the door to head here tonight that Ryan had finally convinced Jack to stay behind. He wouldn't have been able to put on his best show if Jack had been here—he would have been too busy performing directly to him. He would have lost focus. Possibly missed things that would have been important for him to notice. Like the very real fact that the person who had put him in his very first wig might be getting ready to murder him.

"That's too bad," Justine said. "No one should be alone at a time like this. Especially with that speech you gave. I mean . . . if the killer had been here, that would have really pissed him off, don't you think?"

"Yeah, probably. I wasn't really thinking," Ryan said, edging his way toward the door. "You know I've always had a problem running off at the mouth." He could hear the fear in his own voice. She was absolutely right. Him and his big mouth had signed his own death sentence and hadn't even realized it. Justine was right in front of the only door out of the dressing room. He was trapped. "You know, I really should get going. It was great talking to you. I'll call you soon."

He reached for the knob, but Justine put herself in his way. He let out a shaky breath and probably for the first time in his life, he started to pray. "I need to talk to you about something," she said, undoing the clasp on her purse. "It'll only take a second, I promise."

This was it. No amount of praying would protect him from whatever she was about to pull out. He had to save himself. He shoved his drag mother aside, wrenched the door open, and ran into the hall. The *click-clack* of his heels echoed back at him as he fled toward the outside. But there were other footsteps behind him and closing in fast.

"Sheila, wait! Please!"

"Leave me alone!" he shouted. He barreled toward the exit sign and what he hoped was safety. Once he was outside, he could flag someone down. If he even made it out, that was. The other steps grew closer still and he pushed himself to move faster. Running in stilettos was a bitch. Something he hoped he survived long enough to vow never to do again. Finally he reached the door, threw it outward, and felt freedom at last. But then pain burst in the back of his head. Stars exploded in front of his eyes, and there was a dull *thwack* of something metallic hitting flesh and bone.

Then he was falling, and the darkness engulfed him.

CHAPTER SIXTEEN

J ack wasn't going to let himself worry. It was only—he checked his phone again—quarter to two.

The show was supposed to be over by midnight, which meant that Ryan should have been back over an hour ago. Sure, it was possible they'd all gone out to eat, or something after, but Ryan would have said something. Or answered any of the dozen times Jack had called.

His heart pounded, beating more and more furiously until he had to sit and force himself to calm down. But he knew something was wrong. He could feel it in his bones. His hand trembled as he called Ryan one more time. With every ring he prayed a little harder and when the voicemail kicked in, he resisted the urge to hurl his phone across the room. He needed it. He dialed another number.

Nine-one-one.

It only took the dispatcher a few seconds to pick up, but it felt like it stretched on forever. Each ring could have brought Ryan closer to death.

"Nine-one-one, what is the nature of your emergency?"

Jack swallowed, said the words he had wished he'd never have to. "I think my boyfriend is in trouble."

"Why do you think that, sir?"

"He's a drag queen, and—"

"He was one of the performers tonight?"

"Yes." His voice was shaking as bad as his hands now. What would he do if anything had happened to Ryan? They had only been back together a couple of weeks. And they'd both worked so hard to get to where they were. They needed more time.

"What is your address, sir? I'm sending a unit and I'm going to patch you through to the detective in charge of the case."

"A unit? Why? What's wrong? What happened?"

"The detective will explain everything he can, sir. I just need your address. Please."

Jack collapsed onto the sofa, racked his mind trying to remember exactly what Ryan's address was. His brain was mush, and he could barely figure out his own damn name, but finally, he gave the dispatcher what he hoped was the right information.

"One moment, please."

Silence on the other end of the line. Sweat dribbled onto his hand and he wiped at his forehead. What the fuck had happened? It was taking the detective forever to pick up the line, but Jack knew where he could find out.

He turned on the television again. He'd flipped it on and off a dozen times already.

He wasn't surprised to see the red Breaking News banner flashing across the bottom of the screen, but that didn't stop his heart from plummeting into his stomach.

Please, God. Please no.

He felt the tears before he even realized he was crying. It took everything in him not to let sobs overtake him.

"Police are still working to identify the victim," the man on the TV said. "But we can report that the deceased is another drag performer, which means it's likely that the Sapphire Bay Slasher has struck again."

Jack was shaking his head; his bottom lip quivered and he heaved a loud sob that radiated from his soul. This couldn't be happening. He couldn't have lost Ryan. It wasn't fair! He was about to hang up the phone and go to the fucking club himself when a voice came on.

"This is Detective Hart."

"My name is Jack Kieza." Jack wanted to sound composed, but that wasn't happening, so the best he could go for was semiprofessional. If he faked that, maybe he could at least sound normal until he knew Ryan's fate for sure. "My boyfriend was one of the performers at the event at the Reputation Room tonight." His voice cracked. "I'm seeing on the news now that they found another body." Another crack. He didn't want to believe it. And, what was worse, despite everything that had happened, in that moment, he wished his mother was there.

"Your dispatcher said that they were going to send a unit here, and that you would tell me what you could."

The detective was silent for a moment. "I'm sorry to have to ask you this, Mr. Kieza, but can you meet us at the morgue to possibly make an identification?" Morgue. That word dropped into Jack's belly, right next to his heart and sat there. Poisoned him from the inside out. "There were a lot of entertainers there tonight, and if you could make a positive identification, it would help us with other loved ones."

Other loved ones? What about him? What about the one *he* loved? But Jack stifled his outrage. Hopefully the officer hadn't intended to come across as cold as he had. "Yes, of course," he said instead.

A moment later, Jack hung up the phone and sat there. He didn't have any more tears. Not yet, anyway. Instead, numbness had spread over him. He stared at the ground, replaying every moment he'd ever made Ryan unhappy. They'd lost so much time because he hadn't been able to get his shit together. And now, they might not have any more at all.

He was only vaguely aware of the knock at the door a few minutes later. He didn't remember getting up, or walking over. The two uniformed officers standing there when he opened the door looked grim, which only drove the point home further. He was about to see Ryan for the final time. And it wouldn't even be him. Not really. Instead it would just be a shell of the former man.

Jack followed the officers. It was like he was moving through some kind of haze. He didn't remember shutting the door, but even if he hadn't, he wasn't about to turn back to do it. Without Ryan, everything in that house was useless.

They rode the twenty minutes (or maybe two hours, Jack wasn't sure, anymore) to the hospital, and the officers escorted him to the elevator, down to the basement. He knew they were talking to him, but only caught snatches of what they were saying. Something about not being sure who had performed tonight and being grateful about him coming forward. When the doors slid open, the hallway stretched for what looked like miles ahead of him. There were no doors except the double ones at the other end. Dim lighting gave the hall a depressingly final look. Which made sense, he guessed. His feet carried him forward, though he certainly didn't know how to move them. Not anymore. He felt like he was walking to his own death. In a way, that was exactly what he was doing. With every step, his heart grew heavier and heavier. Without Ryan, the best part of his life was over, and they might as well bury him too.

He pushed his way into a much smaller room with a rectangle of glass set against the opposite wall and a door to the right of it. The blinds on the other side of the window were drawn, hiding whatever was in that other room from his view. The smell of disinfectant assaulted him from every side. A man stood next to the window in a plain black suit and red tie. Of course it would be the color of blood.

"Mr. Kieza?" the man asked.

"Yes." Jack kept his eyes trained on that window. He didn't want to be here anymore. He didn't want to see Ryan's body on the other side. But he had to. He would never be able to live with himself if he didn't. So he had to suck it up, and let this be the last memory he had of the man he loved.

"I'm Detective Hart," the man said, holding out a hand. Jack shook it absently. "I'm sorry to meet under these circumstances."

"I want to see him." Jack's voice was thin, barely more than a whisper. He couldn't put it off any longer. This was a bandage he was just going to have to rip away.

"Of course." The detective knocked on the glass and, a moment later, the blinds went up.

Jack stepped forward until he was staring right into the other room. A body lay on the table, covered by a sheet. A pair of hands appeared, pulled the sheet down to the chest. Jack let out another watery sob. His hand flew to his mouth and he stared at the detective, though he could hardly see him through his tears.

"Mr. Kieza." The detective sounded much more sympathetic now than he had on the phone. "Can you identify this man?"

"No," Jack said, smiling wildly. He must have looked insane. It was a shitty reaction, but he couldn't help it. "That's not Ryan. I've never seen that man before."

CHAPTER SEVENTEEN

The back of Ryan's head throbbed, a symphony of pain that made him wish he was dead. But when he tried to put a hand to the aching area and couldn't move it past his shoulder, the last few hours came back to him, piece by piece. The show. Justine. Running away. Justine hitting him and knocking him out.

He opened his eyes at last and saw that he was tied to a chair. He jumped as a silky wave of hair whispered over his shoulder. He was still in drag. And tied up. With a fucking killer on the loose. Oh God. He took it all back. He didn't wish he was dead. This pain was nothing he couldn't deal with. A few Advil and he'd be good as new. He looked around the room he found himself in, vision swimming in and out of focus. It was dark, except for a single dome light above him, which cast an illuminated circle a few feet around him, but that was it. Outside of that, he was totally blind.

How long had he been unconscious? Jack had to be worried sick, and despite his predicament and his terror, Ryan was overwhelmed with guilt at leaving him like this.

"It's about time you woke up," a voice came from the shadows. Ryan's head snapped in that direction and he squinted, trying to force the room to stop dancing around him. He was sure he recognized the voice, but it didn't sound like Justine. Too deep. So who the fuck was it?

He closed his eyes, took a deep breath. When he opened them again, he felt a little more focused. His vision was still shaky around the edges, but the entire room wasn't doing the hokey-pokey anymore. At least for now. "Who's there?"

"Oh come on, bitch. You know the answer to that." Ryan definitely knew that voice. But he was still too foggy to place it. "You just spent all night performing for me. Because you wanted me to see. Wanted me to know that you're *brave*, right? And then you made that speech. Fuck me, right? Isn't that what you said?"

He stepped out of the shadows then, and Ryan felt like he'd been clubbed in the head all over again.

Mike stood in front of him, inspecting him through entirely too calm eyes. This couldn't be right. He had to be hallucinating. No way had his brother murdered five people—five of his *friends*—in cold blood. He'd gotten hit pretty hard. Concussions made you see things that weren't really there, right?

His brother's name was on the tip of his tongue, he meant to say it, but instead what came out was, "Where's Justine?"

"Who's Justine? The bitch who followed you out?" Ryan didn't want to know the answer anymore. But he didn't seem to have a choice. Mike shrugged. "You were the only one who was supposed to die tonight, but he saw me hit you. So I gutted him and cut his throat open." Mike chuckled. "I recognized him; though, he didn't look like that when he came in. I saw him go into the bathroom before you went on stage and when he came out . . ." Mike shook his head. "He begged for his life. Said he had cancer, or something. Made it so much better when I took it away from him."

Ryan's gut twisted with shame. He'd suspected Justine, and she was dead because of it.

That upped the count to six. Mike had killed six people and he was standing there talking about it like it was something normal people did every day. Ryan was going to be sick. He never would have guessed this. Not in a million years. Mike's words from that night Ryan and Jack had run into him floated back to him.

"You'll never know what hit you."

Truer words had never been spoken.

"You know what's funny, though?" Mike knelt in front of Ryan. "Tonight wasn't the first time I saw you. I've been watching you for a while now. And as spunky as you are, I thought I was gonna have to hit you a few times to knock you out. But you went down easy."

Ryan realized with a shock that in his brother's mind, he was talking to Sheila. That he didn't recognize him at all.

"Because you hit me with a fucking brick."

Mike's eye twitched, almost as though he'd recognized Ryan's voice, but a second later any sign of possible realization was gone. "It wasn't a brick. It was a metal pipe. I thought a brick might have killed you too fast, and I wanted to savor this. You wanted to fuck with me, so now I want to make you suffer."

Tears stung Ryan's eyes. "Suffer?" He scoffed. "You've spent the last four months killing my friends. Don't you think you've made me suffer enough?"

"No," Mike said simply. He stood upright, and then Ryan was staring up into his brother's face. Mike's face would be the last one he ever saw. "It's not enough until I say it's enough. And after tonight? It's not going to be enough for a long time." He snarled. "I might keep you here. Bring them all back so you can see what I do to them. Save you for last."

Ryan's bottom lip quivered. There was only one question left. It didn't matter at this point, but he had to know. "Why them? Why us? What did we ever do to you?"

The corners of Mike's mouth turned up in a smile. "Why not?" Ryan felt the air drain out of the room. What kind of answer was that? He squatted again. "Truth be told I didn't care who it was. I just felt like killing someone that night. And your little friend was in the alley. I was only trying to tell him that it wasn't safe to walk in dark alleys at night, and he started mouthing off. So I made sure he couldn't anymore." He shrugged. "Because I could." A dreamy look passed over his face, like he was reliving it. "And I liked the way he bled, so I went after another. And another. Guess you could say I have a type."

Ryan couldn't believe what he was hearing. What kind of psycho shit was this? To think that people woke up and decided that they wanted to kill, then picked a person at random and took them out, all because they could? He wished he hadn't asked.

Mike stood up again.

"I got so hard when the light left their eyes . . . God, I wanted to fuck their corpses. Only reason I didn't was because leaving DNA behind is what gets people caught." Ryan could practically see the idea click into his brain. "I might just fuck you while I tell you exactly what I did to all of them. At least you can put up more of a fight than they would have." He smiled, and Ryan had never seen anything so demented. "I just . . . I fell in love with killing and they were such easy targets."

"God, Mike, I don't want to hear anymore!" He hadn't meant to call him by his name. It had slipped out and now that it had, there was nothing he could do to take it back.

Mike cocked his head to the side and studied Ryan a moment. "How do you know my name?"

Part of Ryan wished that telling his brother who he really was would save him, but the other rational part reminded him that he knew too much. There was no way he was walking out of this room alive. But if he was going to go out, he might as well go out as the real him, right? "Because, Mikey . . . it's me. It's Ryan."

There was that eye twitch again and Mike's eyes searched his face. "Bullshit. Ryan would never . . ."

"I swear, man. Take off the wig. Wipe away the makeup and you'll see that it really is me. Rainey..."

Mike didn't look like he trusted it. He stuck out a hesitant hand, paused just shy of touching the hair. Ryan's heart hammered in his chest. This was a terrible idea, but what other option did he have? Mike snatched the wig away, pulling half a dozen bobby pins and the stocking cap away with it. And there was that exposed feeling he always felt when Sheila started to turn back into Ryan. Only this time, the stakes were way higher than a little depression at the end of the night. Mike still didn't look convinced. He pulled a bloody rag from his pocket, and Ryan realized with a jolt of revulsion that the blood of every queen Mike had murdered was probably hovering mere inches away from his face.

Then it was *on* his face, the scratchy cloth wiping away his makeup. God, it smelled like piss and who the fuck knew what else. Ryan couldn't hold his dinner in. He gagged and puked down the front of his dress. But something as simple as his brother almost tossing his cookies all over him didn't seem to deter Mike in the slightest. And now the smell of vomit and vodka mingled with the others, and Ryan retched again, trying like hell to keep the rest of whatever was in his stomach down.

After a minute, Mike pulled the rag away and Sheila with it. Ryan's face burned in spots it had been scrubbed harder than others, but he looked up and saw Mike backing away, the facts finally staring right at him. His face was a mask of repulsion, and he looked like he was about to be sick himself.

"You . . ." he said. "You . . . you . . ."

Ryan didn't know what he was trying to say, but he seized the opportunity to try to save his own life. "Look, I'm sorry I never told you I did drag. It's just the way Dad reacted the first time he saw me in heels, I was afraid everyone else would be the same, so I kept it to myself. But we're brothers, and you can trust me because I would never turn—" Mike's fist to his jaw put a stop to the words tumbling from Ryan's mouth in that continuous rush. Ryan's head snapped to the side and he stayed like that, fighting back tears. This couldn't be happening.

But it was. He was about to be murdered by his brother, and there wasn't a damn thing he could do about it.

"You lying fucking tranny." Punches started raining down on Ryan as he dared look back at Mike. His eye. His nose. His cheek. His lip. His throat. Every inch of Ryan's face that Mike could reach he was punching over and over again. The chair slid with the force of each blow, and Ryan felt his skin splitting, saw droplets of blood flying in every direction. He tilted backward and Mike followed him down. When he hit the ground, the chair gave a little more as the ropes slid up to a thinner part of the back. Mike seemed to realize it too, because he wrenched the chair from beneath Ryan.

Ryan only had a second to think about trying to run before the chair came down against his midsection, again and again. It had to be made of wood, because it splintered with every blow. Every time Mike shouted, the phrase was punctuated by the chair's wide arch reaching its end against Ryan's body.

"Fucking tranny!" *Wack.* "Always trying to trick people!" *Wack.* "Why can't you just be a man?" *Wack.* This time the chair broke against Ryan, and there was a clatter as Mike threw it aside. Ryan tried to open his eyes, but couldn't see a thing. They were swollen shut. The only sound in the now-silent room was his own sobbing and his brother's harsh breathing. "You're fucking dead," Mike said, every word dripping with disgust. "Say hi to your little fucking friends."

Mike was coming at him again. Ryan's entire body screamed in agony, but somehow he managed get his knees up toward his chest.

Mike's fleshy stomach collided with his heels. His brother grunted in pain, and Ryan kicked as hard as he could. He heard Mike stumble backward, lose his balance, and go down. But something seemed to break his fall. Mike let out a surprised-sounding yelp, groaned, and fell silent. Had he fallen on a piece of the chair?

Ryan listened frantically in case Mike was about to launch another attack, but there was nothing. Something that might have been water hit the ground a few inches away from him in a steady dribble. He wanted to move.

Drip.

But he couldn't. There wasn't a single part of him that didn't ache. How many broken bones did he have?

Drop.

He tried to speak, to call for his phone so it could call the police for him. They could trace the call and figure out where he was. But no sound came out, just a thin, rasping breath and a pain that made fresh tears explode in his eyes.

Drip.

So how was anybody supposed to find him? He could only assume that his brother had hit his head and knocked himself out when he fell, because there was still near-total silence around him. Almost deafening. How had he *maybe* survived all that just to die because no one would come to his rescue before Mike woke up to finish the job?

Drop.

Ryan couldn't think anymore. It hurt to even breathe. But a semicomforting daze was spreading over him. He just wanted to rest for a minute, and he could try to figure out a way to escape when he woke up again.

Drip. Drop. Drip. Drop.

This time, he gave in to the darkness.

CHAPTER EIGHTEEN

Ten days Ryan had been unconscious.

Jack had been by his side every second he could. The only time he'd left had been to shower and work. He wondered, again, what would have happened if they hadn't gotten there in time.

The queen on the table had turned out to be a performer called Justine. A few other queens had identified her after the fact. But as Jack had stood in the morgue with tears of relief streaming down his face, his temporary joy had been overshadowed by the fact that they didn't know where Ryan was. It was then that the court order had come through and the detective had been able to get the phone company to track Ryan's phone, which had led them to the basement of an abandoned building.

Jack recognized the purse by the door as Sheila's at once. They'd made him stay outside, but a few minutes later the paramedics arrived and, a long time after that, they finally wheeled out two men. One was Ryan, beaten bloody, unconscious with an oxygen mask over his face. The paramedic tried to shoo Jack away, but he wasn't having it.

"This is my boyfriend," he said. "And I'll be damned if you're taking him anywhere without me."

"Then you need to come on," the man said as he and one of his teammates loaded Ryan into the back of the ambulance. Jack chanced a glance back to the second body. Even though he had been zipped up tight in a body bag, Jack knew it had to be the killer. Who could have done that to Ryan's face? It looked like there had been such . . . rage.

"Sir! Are you coming, or not?"

Jack wanted to know, desperately, who was in that bag, but he needed to be with Ryan. Before long, the bastard's name and picture would be on every major news station. And sure enough, before the next morning the press broke the story, and Jack was shocked to see Ryan's brother staring back at him from the TV. That was when he stopped paying attention to all of it.

Ryan was alive, and the fucker who'd tried to kill him wasn't. That was all that mattered. But he made it a point to find out as much as he could about what happened in that room. Whatever Ryan had done, however he'd overpowered Mike, when Mike had hit the ground, he'd fallen on an upturned piece of wood that had pierced his heart. A lightning strike of luck if Jack ever saw one, but it had happened and it had probably saved Ryan's life.

Jack's insides twisted as he looked at Ryan now. The swelling in his face had gone down, but it had taken on that deep purple bruises get when they're trying to heal. The top of his head had been completely wrapped in gauze, because in addition to the concussion he'd gotten when Mike had hit him, during their final scuffle, Ryan's head had hit the ground pretty hard and a good amount of flesh had been scraped away. Every one of his ribs on the left side was either broken or fractured, and he'd had a huge gash across his stomach. It was a wonder he hadn't bled out before they'd gotten there, Jack realized again, fighting back yet another round of tears. He was tired of crying, but he couldn't help it.

He just wanted Ryan to wake up, to be able to look into his eyes one more time. But even if he did—and the doctors had made sure that Jack knew there was a fair chance that he might not—his life would never be the same. But regardless, Jack would be by his side the entire time.

"Jack?" The voice came behind him. Jack looked up, wiping away tears that weren't there. He turned around to find both of Ryan's parents standing behind him. They'd been there every day, and Jack was grateful for that, because it meant that he didn't have to deal with this completely alone.

"Hey, Mr. Swift. Mrs. Swift."

His pain was significant, sure, but he couldn't imagine what they must be going through. One son fighting for his life because of their other son who was now dead. The two of them had had news vans parked outside of their house and then their hotel since the morning after. He wondered if at least part of the reason they came so often was so they could get a little peace.

"How is he?" Mrs. Swift asked, crossing the room. She put a hand on her son's shoulder.

"He was moving a little, earlier, but not much has changed other than that."

"But that's progress," she said, something like hope in her voice.

Mr. Swift stood against the wall opposite the bed, like he always did. He looked down at the bed, his expression mournful, just like always. The man was only sixty, to Ryan's thirty-five, but every time he came into this room, he appeared to have aged another ten years.

"This is my fault," he whispered. Jack agreed. But he made sure he didn't betray any sign of that. "If I had just accepted him sooner . . . opened my eyes . . . none of this would have ever happened . . ."

Jack pulled him into a hug. They both needed it. "You can't blame yourself for what other people do," he said as Ryan's father sobbed into the crook of his neck. Jack had spent much of the last week doing just that, but they needed to be strong and united right now so that if—*no, not if. When*—Ryan woke up, he was surrounded by faces that loved him.

A tiny gasp from the other side of the room had Jack turning around. He was ready to ask Ryan's mother what was wrong, but the words died on his lips. Ryan's eyes were open. One of them was blood red, but they were open, and Jack couldn't even begin to put into words the joy that swelled through him in that moment. He ran to the door, tripping over his own feet and righting himself as he held on to the doorjamb. "He's awake!" he cried to the nurses at the station across the hall. He didn't even bother waiting to see what they did. Already, he was back at Ryan's side, looking down at him with tears of joy streaming down his face.

"Hey," he whispered, resisting the mighty urge to caress him. Ryan opened his mouth as though he was going to try to speak, but Jack shook his head. "Don't try to talk. Not yet."

People filed in behind him and he got out of the way so they could do their jobs. Jack tucked himself into the corner, pressing a hand to his mouth. He wanted to collapse, to finally release everything he'd been holding in for the last nine days but, even though there was now a wall of people separating them, he needed to keep his eyes on Ryan, to make sure nothing went wrong and they were really out of the woods before he let that happen. He'd slip away later and collapse in private. But for now, he watched as people checked vitals and charts and fawned over Ryan. And Jack knew that if the circumstances were different and he wasn't lying in a hospital bed with half his body broken, Ryan would have loved every second of it.

But at least Jack could appreciate the sight for now. It was the most beautiful thing he'd ever seen.

EPILOGUE

Six Months Later

After all had been said and done, Ryan had spent nearly twelve weeks in the hospital getting poked and prodded and tested, and relearning how to use his body. Jack had been there the entire time and, when they'd been alone again at last, Jack had explained everything that had happened since he'd lost consciousness that night. Including the fact that he'd won over the judge in Stephanie Benning's case. She hadn't wanted her job back and, instead, the judge had ordered the company to pay her a *very* generous settlement in addition to her legal bills.

Ryan still hadn't been cleared to go back to work, but he'd been going stir-crazy in the house and he could walk, damn it, so he'd begged Jack to take him to the office. What had happened to him had made the news—he'd been labeled a hero for stopping the Slasher— and as the elevator doors had slid open and he'd adjusted his crutches, he'd been met with applause and cheers. He'd looked up, stunned. The entire firm crowded in front of him. A sea of his colleagues, his subordinates, his bosses. A room full of people he respected more than life itself, and they'd all been there, clapping and screaming for him. They didn't care that he was a drag queen. They'd only cared that he was safe, and damn if he hadn't begged Jack to let him stay on the elevator because he had been about to start ugly crying and nobody would want to see that.

He'd be able to go back to work before long, and he'd been assured that his job would be right there where he left it the minute he was ready to return. But now, as he stared at himself in the mirror, he smiled, because even though he loved his job, what he was about to do was far more important.

"Stop being like that," he said, grinning up at Jack. "I'm not made of glass." He jerked his head toward the puff in Jack's hand. "I could have gotten a dozen other people to do this, but I wanted you. Don't make me regret that. Beat my fucking face."

A poor choice of words, as flashes of his face *actually* being beaten rushed in on him, but he shook them away. That was why he was doing this. He wasn't about to let Mike's ghost control him even a minute longer. He'd done most of his own makeup, but he still got wiped pretty quickly, and he needed to save some of his energy, so that was part of why he had Jack pushing the setting powder into every inch of his face and neck. He wouldn't be moving a lot tonight, but the lights in Neon Trees were super fucking bright. And the four and a half minutes Ryan usually spent under them got hot.

Finally, he was satisfied and told Jack he could stop. "Now grab the wig." It was something he could have done himself, but this was bringing him and Jack closer together somehow. Considering he was going to officially ask his boyfriend to move in with him at the end of the night, they needed their relationship to become as strong as possible.

Jack pulled the wig, a curly red number, off the foam head and held it over Ryan's. "Don't worry about it being perfect," Ryan said. "Cuz I'm going to have to wind up doing a couple things to it anyway. But . . ." He grabbed the stocking cap off the table in front of him and stretched it over his head. "What you're going to want to do is try to get those pins through the holes in the cap, because they're going to grip my real hair, and that's what keeps the wig from sliding off."

As Jack did what he was told and bobby pins tugged at Ryan's hair and slid across his scalp, Ryan pulled the lace attached to the end of the wig as straight as it would go and added a little spirit gum. It needed to lay flat on his forehead so no one would see it. There were clips attached to the inside of the wig, as well, one at the back and one on either side. When Jack backed away, his task done, Ryan secured them to the bottoms of the cap, put on a little lipstick and gloss, and gave himself a final once-over.

Sheila was back, damn it, and she'd never looked more stunning, in her not-so-humble opinion. She slipped the sleeves of the dress she'd already put on back over her shoulders and stood up, reaching for her crutches. "You ready?"

Jack looked at her, confused. "What do you mean?"

"I mean you're coming out there with me. We're making this debut together. At least, if that's okay with you."

"Of course it is," Jack said, grinning. He kissed her and when he backed away, his lips glistened with a faint red tint.

Sheila shook her head, the corners of her mouth turning up, and reapplied.

It took her longer than she liked to get from the dressing room to the back of the stage, and she had to take a minute to catch her breath, but it was nothing she hadn't expected. She signaled Rudy that she was ready, and the stage manager turned away, speaking into his headset. The club's overhead music faded away, and Sheila heard the voice of one of the few girls left from the original bunch of performers—Jade. She sent up a word of prayer for her fallen sisters and took a deep breath.

"Ladies and gentlemen and everyone in between of Neon Trees," Jade screamed. "Put your hands together and welcome back to the stage the one! The only! Sheila motherfucking Saltue!"

The roar was deafening, but Sheila lived for it. Never one to keep her fans waiting, she led the way onto the stage, Jack's hand gently at the small of her back. She stared out at the crowd, gratitude swelling inside her. The house was packed from end to end, and every single person was on their feet, looking at her. Hell she even saw a few people from the firm standing out there, cheering her on the same way they had when she'd gone to the office that day. She didn't know how long the crowd cheered and didn't care. Because they were all here for her, and everything she'd done that night, she'd done not only for the other queens, but also people like the ones out there. People who were marginalized. Terrified to be themselves. People like the man next to her had been until he'd come up to her after her show and changed both their lives forever.

She reached down to the pocket of the dress she wore, fingered the square box there. Coming out on stage with her wasn't the only surprise she had in store for Jack tonight.

And standing there beneath the spotlight with the crowd cheering for her and the man she loved at her side, Sheila had never felt more at home.

Dear Reader,

Thank you for reading Brien Michaels's *Anyone But You*!

We know your time is precious and you have many, many entertainment options, so it means a lot that you've chosen to spend your time reading. We really hope you enjoyed it.

We'd be honored if you'd consider posting a review—good or bad—on sites like **Amazon, Barnes & Noble, Kobo, Goodreads, Twitter, Facebook, Tumblr,** and your blog or website. We'd also be honored if you told your friends and family about this book. Word of mouth is a book's lifeblood!

For more information on upcoming releases, author interviews, blog tours, contests, giveaways, and more, please sign up for our weekly, spam-free newsletter and visit us around the web:

Newsletter: riptidepublishing.com/newsletter
Twitter: twitter.com/RiptideBooks
Facebook: facebook.com/RiptidePublishing
Goodreads: tinyurl.com/RiptideOnGoodreads
Tumblr: riptidepublishing.tumblr.com

Thank you so much for Reading the Rainbow!

RiptidePublishing.com

ACKNOWLEDGMENTS

There's a group of men whom I've never met but whose courage to step on stage in a pair of stilettos gave both me and Sheila the courage to keep going with this story. To Billy, Wayne, Alan, Todrick, J, Callum, Matt, Simon, Kyle, Timothy, Kenneth, and all the other actors who have played Lola around the world . . . thank you. Sheila wouldn't have the strength she does if Lola and her Kinky Boots had never run into my life.

ABOUT THE AUTHOR

Brien Michaels was hatched shortly before the turn of the century. He grew up in the DMV area and has been creating characters for as long as he can remember, starting with an imaginary friend named Farquad Beaverhausen. Before turning his considerably wicked imagination to writing, he was an actor, aspiring film student, movie theater concessionist, and the first human to enter the seventy-second dimension. Though it is unclear whether he made it back or if Farquad's evil twin, Brad, has taken control of his body. He's currently on the run from the Secret Police, who want to bring him in for questioning regarding the whereabouts of erotica authors L.A. Witt and Lauren Gallagher. If you encounter him, please contact his publishers immediately, as he likely should be chained to a desk writing and not out walking children in nature.

Enjoy more stories like
Anyone But You
at RiptidePublishing.com!

Too Hot!

Sparks aren't just flying . . .
they're catching.

ISBN: 978-1-62649-860-0

Building Forever

A new town, a new neighbor, and
a new chance to build a forever.

ISBN: 978-1-62649-839-6